Farewell to Manzanar

and Related Readings

McDougal Littell

A HOUGHTON MIFFLIN COMPANY

Evanston, Illinois • Boston • Dallas

Acknowledgments

Houghton Mifflin Company: *Farewell to Manzanar* by Jeanne Wakatsuki Houston and James D. Houston. Copyright © 1973 by James D. Houston. Reprinted by permission of Houghton Mifflin Company. All rights reserved.

Coffee House Press: "The Legend of Superman" and "The Legend of Home" are reprinted from *Legends From Camp* by Lawson Fusao Inada, Coffee House Press, 1993. Copyright © 1993 by Lawson Fusao Inada. Used with permission of Coffee House Press.

HarperCollins Publishers, Inc and Faber and Faber Ltd.: "Sleep in the Mojave Desert," from *Crossing the Water* by Sylvia Plath. Originally appeared in Harper's Magazine. Copyright © 1962 by Sylvia Plath. Reprinted by permission of HarperCollins Publishers, Inc. and Faber and Faber Ltd.

The Nation: "I Remember Pearl Harbor" by Charles Inouye, *The Nation*, December 12, 1988. Reprinted with permission from the December 12, 1988 issue of The Nation magazine.

Hisaye Yamamoto: "Wilshire Bus," from *Seventeen Syllables and Other Stories* by Hisaye Yamamoto, Kitchen Table: Women of Color Press, 1988. Copyright © Hisaye Yamamoto, *Pacific Citizen*, December 1950. Reprinted by permission of the author.

Continued on page 226

Cover illustration by Doug Bowles.
Background photos: top, by Dorothea Lange, National Archives 210-G2-A35; bottom, Library of Congress LCUSF34-72325-D.
Author image by Howard Ikemoto.

Printed in the United States of America.

ISBN 0-395-88455-1

234567—DCI—03 02 01 00 99 98

Contents

Farewell to Manzanar
*Memories of childhood in
an internment camp for
Japanese Americans*
memoir by Jeanne Wakatsuki Houston
and James D. Houston   5

from **Legends from Camp**
poems by Lawson Fusao Inada

The Legend of Superman
*Some things even Superman
doesn't understand.*   179

The Legend of Home
Home seems so far away.   180

Sleep in the Mojave Desert
An inhospitable place to rest
poem by Sylvia Plath   182

**I Remember Pearl Harbor: Dealing
with the "Problem Race"**
*Why the nation should apologize to
interned Japanese Americans*
essay by Charles Shirō Inouye   184

Wilshire Bus

*A former internee's surprising
reaction to anti-Chinese prejudice*

short story by Hisaye Yamamoto   191

Trains at Night

*In 1930s Mexico, all Chinese are
ordered out, but Mr. Lee finds a place
to hide.*

short story by Alberto Alvaro Ríos   198

Visiting Home

*An African-American family is
displaced from their Louisiana farm.*

poem by Kevin Young   208

from Unto the Sons

*What was it like to grow up Italian-
American during World War II?*

memoir by Gay Talese   212

Lectures on How You Never Lived
Back Home

*A multiple identity: smart American
girl, beautiful Filipina, dutiful
daughter*

short story by M. Evelina Galang   221

Farewell to Manzanar

Jeanne Wakatsuki Houston
and
James D. Houston

To the Memory of
KO and RIKU WAKATSUKI
and
WOODROW M. WAKATSUKI

Foreword

When we first considered writing a book about the internment of Japanese Americans during World War Two, we told a New York writer friend about the idea. He said, "It's a dead issue. These days you can hardly get people to read about a live issue. People are issued out."

"I know it," my husband said. "I'm issued out myself. The issue isn't what we want to write about. Everybody knows an injustice was done. How many know what actually went on inside? If they think anything, they think concentration camps. But that conjures up Poland and Siberia. And these camps weren't like that at all."

So we set out to write about the life inside one of those camps—Manzanar—where my family spent three and a half years. We began with a tape recorder and an old 1944 yearbook put together at Manzanar High School. It documented the entire camp scene—the graduating seniors, the guard towers, the Judo pavilion, the creeks I used to wade in, my family's barracks. As the photos brought that world back, I began to dredge up feelings that had lain submerged since the forties. I began to make connections I had previously been afraid to see. It had taken me twenty-five years to reach the point where I could talk openly about Manzanar, and the more I talked, the clearer it became that any book we wrote would have to include a good deal more than day-to-day life inside the compound. To tell what I knew and felt about it would mean telling something about our family before the war, and the years that followed the war, and about my father's past, as well as my own way of seeing things now. Writing it has been a way of coming to terms with the impact these years have had on my entire life.

To complete this book we have had to rely on a good deal besides my own recollections. Many people helped make it possible, more than we can name here. We are especially grateful to all the members of the family who shared their memories, and to these friends: Jack and Mary Takayanagi, Don Tanzawa, and Mary Duffield. We are indebted to the numerous writers and researchers whose works have been indispensable to our own perspective on the period. And we thank the University of California at Santa Cruz for a research grant that made it possible to begin.

Because this is a true story, involving an extraordinary episode in American history, we have included a list of dates and laws we hope will make it easier to follow. It needs some historical context. But this is not political history. It is a story, or a web of stories—my own, my father's, my family's—tracing a few paths, out of the multitude of paths that led up to and away from the experience of the internment.

JEANNE WAKATSUKI HOUSTON

Santa Cruz, California
March 1973

A Chronology

1869 The first Japanese to settle on the U.S. mainland arrive at Gold Hill, near Sacramento, California.

1870 U.S. Congress grants naturalization rights to free whites and people of African descent, omitting mention of Oriental races.

1886 The Japanese government lifts its ban on emigration, allowing its citizens for the first time to make permanent moves to other countries.

1911 U.S. Bureau of Immigration and Naturalization orders that declarations of intent to file for citizenship can only be received from whites and from people of African descent, thus allowing courts to refuse naturalization to the Japanese.

1913 Alien Land Bill prevents Japanese aliens from owning land in California.

1924 Congress passes an Immigration Act stating that no alien ineligible for citizenship shall be admitted to the U.S. This stops all immigration from Japan.

1941 December 7: Surprise attack on Pearl Harbor by the Japanese.

1942 February 19: President Roosevelt signs Executive Order 9066, giving the War Department authority to define military areas in the western states and to exclude from them anyone who might threaten the war effort.

1942   March 25: Evacuees begin to arrive at Manzanar Camp, in Owens Valley, California, the first of the permanent camps to open.

1942   August 12: Evacuation completed, 110,000 people of Japanese ancestry removed from the west coast to ten inland camps.

1944   December 18: U.S. Supreme Court rules that loyal citizens cannot be held in detention camps against their will, the first major step toward the closing of the camps.

1945   August 14: Japan surrenders, ending World War II.

1945   November 21: Manzanar Camp officially closes.

1952   June: Congress passes Public Law 414, granting Japanese aliens the right to become naturalized U.S. citizens.

TERMS USED IN THIS BOOK

Issei The first generation. The Issei were born in Japan. Most of them immigrated to the United States between 1890 and 1915.

Nisei The second generation, the children of the Issei. American citizens by birth, almost all Nisei were born before the Second World War.

Sansei The third generation of Americans with Japanese ancestry, most of them born during or after the Second World War.

It is sobering to recall that though the Japanese relocation program, carried through at such incalculable cost in misery and tragedy, was justified on the ground that the Japanese were potentially disloyal, the record does not disclose a single case of Japanese disloyalty or sabotage during the whole war . . .

HENRY STEELE COMMAGER
Harper's Magazine, 1947

Life has left her footprints on my forehead
But I have become a child again this morning
The smile, seen through leaves and flowers,
    is back, to smooth
Away the wrinkles
As the rains wipe away footprints
    on the beach. Again a
Cycle of birth and death begins.

THICH NHAT HANH
Viet Nam Poems (1967)

PART ONE

Chapter 1

"What Is Pearl Harbor?"

On that first weekend in December there must have been twenty or twenty-five boats getting ready to leave. I had just turned seven. I remember it was Sunday because I was out of school, which meant I could go down to the wharf and watch. In those days—1941—there was no smog around Long Beach. The water was clean, the sky a sharp Sunday blue, with all the engines of that white sardine fleet puttering up into it, and a lot of yelling, especially around Papa's boat. Papa loved to give orders. He had attended military school in Japan until the age of seventeen, and part of him never got over that. My oldest brothers, Bill and Woody, were his crew. They would have to check the nets again, and check the fuel tanks again, and run back to the grocery store for some more cigarettes, and then somehow everything had been done, and they were easing away from the wharf, joining the line of boats heading out past the lighthouse, into the harbor.

Papa's boat was called *The Nereid*—long, white, low-slung, with a foredeck wheel cabin. He had another smaller boat, called *The Waka* (a short version of our name), which he kept in Santa Monica, where we lived. But *The Nereid* was his pride. It was worth about $25,000 before the war, and the way he stood in the cabin steering toward open water you would think the whole fleet was under his command. Papa had a mustache then. He wore knee-high rubber boots, a rust-colored turtleneck Mama had knitted him, and a black skipper's hat. He liked to hear himself called "Skipper."

Through one of the big canneries he had made a deal to pay for *The Nereid* with percentages of each catch, and he was anxious to get it paid off. He didn't much like working for someone else if he could help it. A lot of fishermen around San Pedro Harbor had similar contracts with the canneries. In typical Japanese fashion, they all wanted to be independent commercial fishermen, yet they almost always fished together. They would take off from Terminal Island, help each other find the schools of sardine, share nets and radio equipment—competing and cooperating at the same time.

You never knew how long they'd be gone, a couple of days, sometimes a week, sometimes a month, depending on the fish. From the wharf we waved goodbye—my mother, Bill's wife, Woody's wife Chizu, and me. We yelled at them to have a good trip, and after they were out of earshot and the sea had swallowed their engine noises, we kept waving. Then we just stood there with the other women, watching. It was a kind of duty, perhaps a way of adding a little good luck to the voyage, or warding off the bad. It was also marvelously warm, almost summery, the way December days can be sometimes in southern California. When the boats came back, the women who lived on Terminal Island would be rushing to the canneries. But for the moment there wasn't much else to do. We watched until the boats became a row of tiny white gulls on the horizon. Our vigil would end when they slipped over the edge and disappeared. You had to squint against the glare to keep them sighted, and with every blink you expected the last white speck to be gone.

But this time they didn't disappear. They kept floating out there, suspended, as if the horizon had finally become what it always seemed to be from shore: the sea's limit, beyond which no man could sail. They floated awhile, then they began to grow, tiny gulls becoming boats again, a white armada cruising toward us.

"They're coming back," my mother said.

"Why would they be coming back?" Chizu said.

"Something with the engine."

"Maybe somebody got hurt."

"But they wouldn't *all* come back," Mama said, bewildered.

Another woman said, "Maybe there's a storm coming."

They all glanced at the sky, scanning the unmarred horizon. Mama shook her head. There was no explanation. No one had ever seen anything like this before. We watched and waited, and when the boats were still about half a mile off the lighthouse, a fellow from the cannery came running down to the wharf shouting that the Japanese had just bombed Pearl Harbor.

Chizu said to Mama, "What does he mean? What is Pearl Harbor?"

Mama yelled at him, "What is Pearl Harbor?"

But he was running along the docks, like Paul Revere, bringing the news, and didn't have time to explain.

That night Papa burned the flag he had brought with him from Hiroshima thirty-five years earlier. It was such a beautiful piece of material, I couldn't believe he was doing that. He burned a lot of papers too, documents, anything that might suggest he still had some connection with Japan. These precautions didn't do him much good. He was not only an alien; he held a commercial fishing license, and in the early days of the war the FBI was picking up all such men, for fear they were somehow making contact with enemy ships off the coast. Papa himself knew it would only be a matter of time.

They got him two weeks later, when we were staying overnight at Woody's place, on Terminal Island. Five hundred Japanese families lived there then, and FBI deputies had been questioning everyone, ransacking houses for anything that could conceivably be used for signaling planes or ships or that indicated loyalty to the Emperor. Most of the houses had radios with a short-wave band and a high aerial on the roof so that wives could make contact with the fishing boats during these long cruises. To the FBI every radio owner was a potential saboteur. The confiscators were often deputies sworn in hastily during the turbulent days right after Pearl Harbor, and these men seemed to be acting out the general panic, seeing sinister possibilities in the most ordinary household items: flashlights, kitchen knives, cameras, lanterns, toy swords.

If Papa were trying to avoid arrest, he wouldn't have gone near that island. But I think he knew it was futile to hide out or resist. The next morning two FBI men in fedora hats and trench coats—like out of a thirties movie—knocked on Woody's door, and when they left, Papa was between them. He didn't struggle. There was no point to it. He had become a man without a country. The land of his birth was at war with America; yet after thirty-five years here he was still prevented by law from becoming an American citizen. He was suddenly a man with no rights who looked exactly like the enemy.

About all he had left at this point was his tremendous dignity. He was tall for a Japanese man, nearly six feet, lean and hard and healthy-skinned from the sea. He was over fifty. Ten children and a lot of hard luck had worn him down, had worn away most of the arrogance he came to this country with. But he still had dignity, and he would not let those deputies push him out the door. He led them.

Mama knew they were taking all the alien men first to an interrogation center right there on the island. Some were simply being questioned and released. In the beginning she wasn't too worried; at least she wouldn't let herself be. But it grew dark and he wasn't back. Another day went by and we still had heard nothing. Then word came that he had been taken into custody and shipped out. Where to, or for how long? No one knew. All my brothers' attempts to find out were fruitless.

What had they charged him with? We didn't know that either, until an article appeared the next day in the Santa Monica paper, saying he had been arrested for delivering oil to Japanese submarines offshore.

My mother began to weep. It seems now that she wept for days. She was a small, plump woman who laughed easily and cried easily, but I had never seen her cry like this. I couldn't understand it. I remember clinging to her legs, wondering why everyone was crying. This was the beginning of a terrible, frantic time for all my family. But I myself didn't cry about Papa, or have any inkling of what was wrenching Mama's heart, until the next time I saw him, almost a year later.

Chapter 2

Shikata Ga Nai

In December of 1941 Papa's disappearance didn't bother me nearly so much as the world I soon found myself in.

He had been a jack-of-all-trades. When I was born he was farming near Inglewood. Later, when he started fishing, we moved to Ocean Park, near Santa Monica, and until they picked him up, that's where we lived, in a big frame house with a brick fireplace, a block back from the beach. We were the only Japanese family in the neighborhood. Papa liked it that way. He didn't want to be labeled or grouped by anyone. But with him gone and no way of knowing what to expect, my mother moved all of us down to Terminal Island. Woody already lived there, and one of my older sisters had married a Terminal Island boy. Mama's first concern now was to keep the family together; and once the war began, she felt safer there than isolated racially in Ocean Park. But for me, at age seven, the island was a country as foreign as India or Arabia would have been. It was the first time I had lived among other Japanese, or gone to school with them, and I was terrified all the time.

This was partly Papa's fault. One of his threats to keep us younger kids in line was "I'm going to sell you to the Chinaman." When I had entered kindergarten two years earlier, I was the only Oriental in the class. They sat me next to a Caucasian girl who happened to have very slanted eyes. I looked at her and began to scream, certain Papa had sold me out at last. My fear of her ran so deep I could not speak of it, even to Mama, couldn't explain why I was screaming. For two weeks I had nightmares about this girl, until the teachers finally moved me to the other side of the room. And it was still with me, this fear of Oriental faces, when we moved to Terminal Island.

In those days it was a company town, a ghetto owned and controlled by the canneries. The men went after fish, and whenever the boats came back—day or night—the women would be called to process the catch while it was fresh. One in the afternoon or four in the morning, it made no difference. My mother had to go to work right after we moved there. I can still hear the whistle—two toots for French's, three for Van Camp's—and she and Chizu would be out of bed in the middle of the night, heading for the cannery.

The house we lived in was nothing more than a shack, a barracks with single plank walls and rough wooden floors, like the cheapest kind of migrant workers' housing. The people around us were hardworking, boisterous, a little proud of their nickname, *yo-go-re,* which meant literally *uncouth one,* or roughneck, or dead-end kid. They not only spoke Japanese exclusively, they spoke a dialect peculiar to Kyushu, where their families had come from in Japan, a rough, fisherman's language, full of oaths and insults. Instead of saying *ba-ka-ta-re,* a common insult meaning *stupid,* Terminal Islanders would say *ba-ka-ya-ro,* a coarser and exclusively masculine use of the word, which implies gross stupidity. They would swagger and pick on outsiders and persecute anyone who didn't speak as they did. That was what made my own time there so hateful. I had never spoken anything but English, and the other kids in the second grade despised me for it. They were tough and mean, like ghetto kids anywhere. Each day after school I dreaded their ambush. My brother Kiyo, three years older, would wait for me at the door, where we would decide whether to run straight home together, or split up, or try a new and unexpected route.

None of these kids ever actually attacked. It was the threat that frightened us, their fearful looks, and the noises they would make, like miniature Samurai, in a language we couldn't understand.

At the time it seemed we had been living under this reign of fear for years. In fact, we lived there about two months. Late in February the navy decided to clear Terminal Island completely. Even though most of us were American-born, it was dangerous having that many Orientals so close to the Long Beach Naval Station, on the opposite end of the island. We had known something like this was coming. But, like Papa's arrest, not much could be done ahead of time. There were four of us kids still young enough to be living with Mama, plus Granny, her mother, sixty-five then, speaking no English, and nearly blind. Mama didn't know where else she could get work, and we had nowhere else to move *to.* On February 25 the choice was made for us. We were given forty-eight hours to clear out.

The secondhand dealers had been prowling around

for weeks, like wolves, offering humiliating prices for goods and furniture they knew many of us would have to sell sooner or later. Mama had left all but her most valuable possessions in Ocean Park, simply because she had nowhere to put them. She had brought along her pottery, her silver, heirlooms like the kimonos Granny had brought from Japan, tea sets, lacquered tables, and one fine old set of china, blue and white porcelain, almost translucent. On the day we were leaving, Woody's car was so crammed with boxes and luggage and kids we had just run out of room. Mama had to sell this china.

One of the dealers offered her fifteen dollars for it. She said it was a full setting for twelve and worth at least two hundred. He said fifteen was his top price. Mama started to quiver. Her eyes blazed up at him. She had been packing all night and trying to calm down Granny, who didn't understand why we were moving again and what all the rush was about. Mama's nerves were shot, and now navy jeeps were patrolling the streets. She didn't say another word. She just glared at this man, all the rage and frustration channeled at him through her eyes.

He watched her for a moment and said he was sure he couldn't pay more than seventeen fifty for that china. She reached into the red velvet case, took out a dinner plate and hurled it at the floor right in front of his feet.

The man leaped back shouting, "Hey! Hey, don't do that! Those are valuable dishes!"

Mama took out another dinner plate and hurled it at the floor, then another and another, never moving, never opening her mouth, just quivering and glaring at the retreating dealer, with tears streaming down her cheeks. He finally turned and scuttled out the door, heading for the next house. When he was gone she stood there smashing cups and bowls and platters until the whole set lay in scattered blue and white fragments across the wooden floor.

The American Friends Service helped us find a small house in Boyle Heights, another minority ghetto, in downtown Los Angeles, now inhabited briefly by a few hundred Terminal Island refugees. Executive Order 9066 had been signed by President Roosevelt, giving the War Department authority to define military areas in the western states and to exclude from them anyone who might threaten the war effort. There was a lot of talk about internment, or moving inland, or something like that in store for all Japanese Americans. I remember my brothers sitting around the table talking very intently about what we were going to do, how we would keep the family together. They had seen how quickly Papa was removed, and they knew now that he would not be back for quite a while. Just before leaving Terminal Island Mama had received her first letter, from Bismarck, North Dakota. He had been imprisoned at Fort Lincoln, in an all-male camp for enemy aliens.

Papa had been the patriarch. He had always decided everything in the family. With him gone, my brothers, like councilors in the absence of a chief, worried about what should be done. The ironic thing is, there wasn't much left to decide. These were mainly days of quiet, desperate waiting for what seemed at the time to be inevitable. There is a phrase the Japanese use in such situations, when something difficult must be endured. You would hear the older heads, the Issei, telling others very quietly, *"Shikata ga nai"* (It cannot be helped). *"Shikata ga nai"* (It must be done).

Mama and Woody went to work packing celery for

a Japanese produce dealer. Kiyo and my sister May and I enrolled in the local school, and what sticks in my memory from those few weeks is the teacher—not her looks, her remoteness. In Ocean Park my teacher had been a kind, grandmotherly woman who used to sail with us in Papa's boat from time to time and who wept the day we had to leave. In Boyle Heights the teacher felt cold and distant. I was confused by all the moving and was having trouble with the classwork, but she would never help me out. She would have nothing to do with me.

This was the first time I had felt outright hostility from a Caucasian. Looking back, it is easy enough to explain. Public attitudes toward the Japanese in California were shifting rapidly. In the first few months of the Pacific war, America was on the run. Tolerance had turned to distrust and irrational fear. The hundred-year-old tradition of anti-Orientalism on the west coast soon resurfaced, more vicious than ever. Its result became clear about a month later, when we were told to make our third and final move.

The name Manzanar meant nothing to us when we left Boyle Heights. We didn't know where it was or what it was. We went because the government ordered us to. And, in the case of my older brothers and sisters, we went with a certain amount of relief. They had all heard stories of Japanese homes being attacked, of beatings in the streets of California towns. They were as frightened of the Caucasians as Caucasians were of us. Moving, under what appeared to be government protection, to an area less directly threatened by the war seemed not such a bad idea at all. For some it actually sounded like a fine adventure.

Our pickup point was a Buddhist church in Los Angeles. It was very early, and misty, when we got there with our luggage. Mama had bought heavy coats for all of us. She grew up in eastern Washington and knew that anywhere inland in early April would be cold. I was proud of my new coat, and I remember sitting on a duffel bag trying to be friendly with the Greyhound driver. I smiled at him. He didn't smile back. He was befriending no one. Someone tied a numbered tag to my collar and to the duffel bag (each family was given a number, and that became our official designation until the camps were closed), someone else passed out box lunches for the trip, and we climbed aboard.

I had never been outside Los Angeles County, never traveled more than ten miles from the coast, had never even ridden on a bus. I was full of excitement, the way any kid would be, and wanted to look out the window. But for the first few hours the shades were drawn. Around me other people played cards, read magazines, dozed, waiting. I settled back, waiting too, and finally fell asleep. The bus felt very secure to me. Almost half its passengers were immediate relatives. Mama and my older brothers had succeeded in keeping most of us together, on the same bus, headed for the same camp. I didn't realize until much later what a job that was. The strategy had been, first, to have everyone living in the same district when the evacuation began, and then to get all of us included under the same family number, even though names had been changed by marriage. Many families weren't as lucky as ours and suffered months of anguish while trying to arrange transfers from one camp to another.

We rode all day. By the time we reached our destination, the shades were up. It was late afternoon. The first thing I saw was a yellow swirl across a blurred, reddish setting sun. The bus was being pelted by what sounded like splattering rain. It wasn't rain. This was my first look at something I would soon know very well, a billowing flurry of dust and sand churned up by the wind through Owens Valley.

We drove past a barbed-wire fence, through a gate, and into an open space where trunks and sacks and packages had been dumped from the baggage trucks that drove out ahead of us. I could see a few tents set up, the first rows of black barracks, and beyond them, blurred by sand, rows of barracks that seemed to spread for miles across this plain. People were sitting on cartons or milling around, with their backs to the wind, waiting to see which friends or relatives might be on this bus. As we approached, they turned or stood up, and some moved toward us expectantly. But inside the bus no one stirred. No one waved or spoke. They just stared out the windows, ominously silent. I didn't understand this. Hadn't we finally arrived, our whole family intact? I opened a window, leaned out, and yelled happily. "Hey! This whole bus is full of Wakatsukis!"

Outside, the greeters smiled. Inside there was an explosion of laughter, hysterical, tension-breaking laughter that left my brothers choking and whacking each other across the shoulders.

We had pulled up just in time for dinner. The mess halls weren't completed yet. An outdoor chow line snaked around a half-finished building that broke a good part of the wind. They issued us army mess kits, the round metal kind that fold over, and plopped in scoops of canned Vienna sausage, canned string beans, steamed rice that had been cooked too long, and on top of the rice a serving of canned apricots. The Caucasian servers were thinking that the fruit poured over rice would make a good dessert. Among the Japanese, of course, rice is never eaten with sweet foods, only with salty or savory foods. Few of us could eat such a mixture. But at this point no one dared protest. It would have been impolite. I was horrified when I saw the apricot syrup seeping through my little mound of rice. I opened my mouth to complain. My mother jabbed me in the back to keep quiet. We moved on through the line and joined the others squatting in the lee of half-raised walls, dabbing courteously at what was, for almost everyone there, an inedible concoction.

After dinner we were taken to Block 16, a cluster of fifteen barracks that had just been finished a day or so earlier—although finished was hardly the word for it. The shacks were built of one thickness of pine planking covered with tarpaper. They sat on concrete footings, with about two feet of open space between the floorboards and the ground. Gaps showed between the planks, and as the weeks passed and the green wood dried out, the gaps widened. Knotholes gaped in the uncovered floor.

Each barracks was divided into six units, sixteen by twenty feet, about the size of a living room, with one bare bulb hanging from the ceiling and an oil stove for heat. We were assigned two of these for the twelve people in our family group; and our official family "number" was enlarged by three digits—16 plus the number of this barracks. We were issued steel army cots, two brown army blankets each, and some mattress covers, which my brothers stuffed with straw.

The first task was to divide up what space we had for sleeping. Bill and Woody contributed a blanket each and partitioned off the first room: one side for Bill and Tomi, one side for Woody and Chizu and their baby girl. Woody also got the stove, for heating formulas.

The people who had it hardest during the first few

months were young couples like these, many of whom had married just before the evacuation began, in order not to be separated and sent to different camps. Our two rooms were crowded, but at least it was all in the family. My oldest sister and her husband were shoved into one of those sixteen-by-twenty-foot compartments with six people they had never seen before— two other couples, one recently married like themselves, the other with two teenage boys. Partitioning off a room like that wasn't easy. It was bitter cold when we arrived, and the wind did not abate. All they had to use for room dividers were those army blankets, two of which were barely enough to keep one person warm. They argued over whose blanket should be sacrificed and later argued about noise at night—the parents wanted their boys asleep by 9:00 p.m.—and they continued arguing over matters like that for six months, until my sister and her husband left to harvest sugar beets in Idaho. It was grueling work up there, and wages were pitiful, but when the call came through camp for workers to alleviate the wartime labor shortage, it sounded better than their life at Manzanar. They knew they'd have, if nothing else, a room, perhaps a cabin of their own.

That first night in Block 16, the rest of us squeezed into the second room—Granny, Lillian, age fourteen, Ray, thirteen, May, eleven, Kiyo, ten, Mama, and me. I didn't mind this at all at the time. Being youngest meant I got to sleep with Mama. And before we went to bed I had a great time jumping up and down on the mattress. The boys had stuffed so much straw into hers, we had to flatten it some so we wouldn't slide off. I slept with her every night after that until Papa came back.

Chapter 3

A Different Kind of Sand

We woke early, shivering and coated with dust that had blown up through the knotholes and in through the slits around the doorway. During the night Mama had unpacked all our clothes and heaped them on our beds for warmth. Now our cubicle looked as if a great laundry bag had exploded and then been sprayed with fine dust. A skin of sand covered the floor. I looked over Mama's shoulder at Kiyo, on top of his fat mattress, buried under jeans and overcoats and sweaters. His eyebrows were gray, and he was starting to giggle. He was looking at me, at my gray eyebrows and coated hair, and pretty soon we were both giggling. I looked at Mama's face to see if she thought Kiyo was funny. She lay very still next to me on our mattress, her eyes scanning everything—bare rafters, walls, dusty kids—scanning slowly, and I think the mask of her face would have cracked had not Woody's voice just then come at us through the wall. He was rapping on the planks as if testing to see if they were hollow.

"Hey!" he yelled. "You guys fall into the same flour barrel as us?"

"No," Kiyo yelled back. "Ours is full of Japs."

All of us laughed at this.

"Well, tell 'em it's time to get up," Woody said. "If we're gonna live in this place, we better get to work."

He gave us ten minutes to dress, then he came in carrying a broom, a hammer, and a sack full of tin can lids he had scrounged somewhere. Woody would be our leader for a while now, short, stocky, grinning behind his mustache. He had just turned twenty-four. In later years he would tour the country with Mr. Moto, the Japanese tag-team wrestler, as his sinister assistant Suki—karate chops through the ropes from outside the ring, a chunky leg reaching from under his kimono to trip up Mr. Moto's foe. In the ring Woody's smile looked sly and crafty; he hammed it up. Offstage it was whimsical, as if some joke were bursting to be told.

"Hey, brother Ray, Kiyo," he said. "You see these tin can lids?"

"Yeah, yeah," the boys said drowsily, as if going back to sleep. They were both young versions of Woody.

"You see all them knotholes in the floor and in the walls?"

They looked around. You could see about a dozen.

Woody said, "You get those covered up before breakfast time. Any more sand comes in here through one of them knotholes, you have to eat it off the floor with ketchup."

"What about sand that comes in through the cracks?" Kiyo said.

Woody stood up very straight, which in itself was funny, since he was only about five-foot-six.

"Don't worry about the cracks," he said. "Different kind of sand comes in through the cracks."

He put his hands on his hips and gave Kiyo a sternly comic look, squinting at him through one eye the way Papa would when he was asserting his authority. Woody mimicked Papa's voice: "And I can tell the difference. So be careful."

The boys laughed and went to work nailing down lids. May started sweeping out the sand. I was helping Mama fold the clothes we'd used for cover, when Woody came over and put his arm around her shoulder. He was short; she was even shorter, under five feet.

He said softly, "You okay, Mama?"

She didn't look at him, she just kept folding clothes and said, "Can we get the cracks covered too, Woody?"

Outside the sky was clear, but icy gusts of wind were buffeting our barracks every few minutes, sending fresh dust puffs up through the floorboards. May's broom could barely keep up with it, and our oil heater could scarcely hold its own against the drafts.

"We'll get this whole place as tight as a barrel, Mama. I already met a guy who told me where they pile all the scrap lumber."

"Scrap?"

"That's all they got. I mean, they're still building the camp, you know. Sixteen blocks left to go. After that, they say maybe we'll get some stuff to fix the insides a little bit."

Her eyes blazed then, her voice quietly furious. "Woody, we can't live like this. Animals live like this."

It was hard to get Woody down. He'd keep smiling when everybody else was ready to explode. Grief flickered in his eyes. He blinked it away and hugged her tighter. "We'll make it better, Mama. You watch."

We could hear voices in other cubicles now. Beyond the wall Woody's baby girl started to cry.

"I have to go over to the kitchen," he said, "see if those guys got a pot for heating bottles. That oil stove takes too long—something wrong with the fuel line. I'll find out what they're giving us for breakfast."

"Probably hotcakes with soy sauce," Kiyo said, on his hands and knees between the bunks.

"No." Woody grinned, heading out the door. "Rice. With Log Cabin Syrup and melted butter."

Chapter 4

A Common Master Plan

I don't remember what we ate that first morning. I know we stood for half an hour in cutting wind waiting to get our food. Then we took it back to the cubicle and ate huddled around the stove. Inside, it was warmer than when we left, because Woody was already making good his promise to Mama, tacking up some ends of lath he'd found, stuffing rolled paper around the door frame.

Trouble was, he had almost nothing to work with. Beyond this temporary weather stripping, there was little else he could do. Months went by, in fact, before our "home" changed much at all from what it was the day we moved in—bare floors, blanket partitions, one bulb in each compartment dangling from a roof beam, and open ceilings overhead so that mischievous boys like Ray and Kiyo could climb up into the rafters and peek into anyone's life.

The simple truth is the camp was no more ready for us when we got there than we were ready for it. We had only the dimmest ideas of what to expect. Most of the families, like us, had moved out from southern

California with as much luggage as each person could carry. Some old men left Los Angeles wearing Hawaiian shirts and Panama hats and stepped off the bus at an altitude of 4000 feet, with nothing available but sagebrush and tarpaper to stop the April winds pouring down off the back side of the Sierras.

The War Department was in charge of all the camps at this point. They began to issue military surplus from the First World War—olive-drab knit caps, earmuffs, peacoats, canvas leggings. Later on, sewing machines were shipped in, and one barracks was turned into a clothing factory. An old seamstress took a peacoat of mine, tore the lining out, opened and flattened the sleeves, added a collar, put arm holes in and handed me back a beautiful cape. By fall dozens of seamstresses were working full-time transforming thousands of these old army clothes into capes, slacks and stylish coats. But until that factory got going and packages from friends outside began to fill out our wardrobes, warmth was more important than style. I couldn't help laughing at Mama walking around in army earmuffs and a pair of wide-cuffed, khaki-colored wool trousers several sizes too big for her. Japanese are generally smaller than Caucasians, and almost all these clothes were oversize. They flopped, they dangled, they hung.

It seems comical, looking back; we were a band of Charlie Chaplins marooned in the California desert. But at the time, it was pure chaos. That's the only way to describe it. The evacuation had been so hurriedly planned, the camps so hastily thrown together, nothing was completed when we got there, and almost nothing worked.

I was sick continually, with stomach cramps and diarrhea. At first it was from the shots they gave us for typhoid, in very heavy doses and in assembly-line fashion: swab, jab, swab, *Move along now*, swab, jab, swab, *Keep it moving.* That knocked all of us younger kids down at once, with fevers and vomiting. Later, it was the food that made us sick, young and old alike. The kitchens were too small and badly ventilated. Food would spoil from being left out too long. That summer, when the heat got fierce, it would spoil faster. The refrigeration kept breaking down. The cooks, in many cases, had never cooked before. Each block had to provide its own volunteers. Some were lucky and had a professional or two in their midst. But the first chef in our block had been a gardener all his life and suddenly found himself preparing three meals a day for 250 people.

"The Manzanar runs" became a condition of life, and you only hoped that when you rushed to the latrine, one would be in working order.

That first morning, on our way to the chow line, Mama and I tried to use the women's latrine in our block. The smell of it spoiled what little appetite we had. Outside, men were working in an open trench, up to their knees in muck—a common sight in the months to come. Inside, the floor was covered with excrement, and all twelve bowls were erupting like a row of tiny volcanoes.

Mama stopped a kimono-wrapped woman stepping past us with her sleeve pushed up against her nose and asked, "What do you do?"

"Try Block Twelve," the woman said, grimacing. "They have just finished repairing the pipes."

It was about two city blocks away. We followed her over there and found a line of women waiting in the wind outside the latrine. We had no choice but to join the line and wait with them.

Inside it was like all the other latrines. Each block was built to the same design, just as each of the ten camps, from California to Arkansas, was built to a common master plan. It was an open room, over a concrete slab. The sink was a long metal trough against one wall, with a row of spigots for hot and cold water. Down the center of the room twelve toilet bowls were arranged in six pairs, back to back, with no partitions. My mother was a very modest person, and this was going to be agony for her, sitting down in public, among strangers.

One old woman had already solved the problem for herself by dragging in a large cardboard carton. She set it up around one of the bowls, like a three-sided screen. OXYDOL was printed in large black letters down the front. I remember this well, because that was the soap we were issued for laundry; later on, the smell of it would permeate these rooms. The upended carton was about four feet high. The old woman behind it wasn't much taller. When she stood, only her head showed over the top.

She was about Granny's age. With great effort she was trying to fold the sides of the screen together. Mama happened to be at the head of the line now. As she approached the vacant bowl, she and the old woman bowed to each other from the waist. Mama then moved to help her with the carton, and the old woman said very graciously, in Japanese, "Would you like to use it?"

Happily, gratefully, Mama bowed again and said, "*Arigato*" (Thank you). "*Arigato gozaimas*" (Thank you very much). "I will return it to your barracks."

"Oh, no. It is not necessary. I will be glad to wait."

The old woman unfolded one side of the cardboard, while Mama opened the other; then she bowed again and scurried out the door.

Those big cartons were a common sight in the spring of 1942. Eventually sturdier partitions appeared, one or two at a time. The first were built of scrap lumber. Word would get around that Block such and such had partitions now, and Mama and my older sisters would walk halfway across the camp to use them. Even after every latrine in camp was screened, this quest for privacy continued. Many would wait until late at night. Ironically, because of this, midnight was often the most crowded time of all.

Like so many of the women there, Mama never did get used to the latrines. It was a humiliation she just learned to endure: *shikata ga nai,* this cannot be helped. She would quickly subordinate her own desires to those of the family or the community, because she knew cooperation was the only way to survive. At the same time she placed a high premium on personal privacy, respected it in others and insisted upon it for herself. Almost everyone at Manzanar had inherited this pair of traits from the generations before them who had learned to live in a small, crowded country like Japan. Because of the first they were able to take a desolate stretch of wasteland and gradually make it livable. But the entire situation there, especially in the beginning—the packed sleeping quarters, the communal mess halls, the open toilets— all this was an open insult to that other, private self, a slap in the face you were powerless to challenge.

Chapter 5

Almost a Family

At seven I was too young to be insulted. The camp worked on me in a much different way. I wasn't aware of this at the time, of course. No one was, except maybe Mama, and there was little she could have done to change what happened.

It began in the mess hall. Before Manzanar, mealtime had always been the center of our family scene. In camp, and afterward, I would often recall with deep yearning the old round wooden table in our dining room in Ocean Park, the biggest piece of furniture we owned, large enough to seat twelve or thirteen of us at once. A tall row of elegant, lathe-turned spindles separated this table from the kitchen, allowing talk to pass from one room to the other. Dinners were always noisy, and they were always abundant with great pots of boiled rice, platters of home-grown vegetables, fish Papa caught.

He would sit at the head of this table, with Mama next to him serving and the rest of us arranged around the edges according to age, down to where Kiyo and I sat, so far away from our parents, it seemed at the time, we had our own enclosed nook inside this world. The grownups would be talking down at their end, while we two played our secret games, making eyes at each other when Papa gave the order to begin to eat, racing with chopsticks to scrape the last grain from our rice bowls, eyeing Papa to see if he had noticed who won.

Now, in the mess halls, after a few weeks had passed, we stopped eating as a family. Mama tried to hold us together for a while, but it was hopeless. Granny was too feeble to walk across the block three times a day, especially during heavy weather, so May brought food to her in the barracks. My older brothers and sisters, meanwhile, began eating with their friends, or eating somewhere blocks away, in the hope of finding better food. The word would get around that the cook over in Block 22, say, really knew his stuff, and they would eat a few meals over there, to test the rumor. Camp authorities frowned on mess hall hopping and tried to stop it, but the good cooks liked it. They liked to see long lines outside their kitchens and would work overtime to attract a crowd.

Younger boys, like Ray, would make a game of seeing how many mess halls they could hit in one meal period—be the first in line at Block 16, gobble down your food, run to 17 by the middle of the dinner hour, gulp another helping, and hurry to 18 to make the end of that chow line and stuff in the third meal of the evening. They didn't *need* to do that. No matter how bad the food might be, you could always eat till you were full.

Kiyo and I were too young to run around, but often we would eat in gangs with other kids, while the grownups sat at another table. I confess I enjoyed this part of it at the time. We all did. A couple of years after the camps opened, sociologists studying the life noticed what had happened to the families. They made some recommendations, and edicts went out that families *must* start eating together again. Most people resented this; they griped and grumbled. They were in the habit of eating with their friends. And until the mess hall system itself could be changed, not much could really be done. It was too late.

My own family, after three years of mess hall living, collapsed as an integrated unit. Whatever dignity or feeling of filial strength we may have known before December 1941 was lost, and we did not recover it until many years after the war, not until after Papa died and we began to come together, trying to fill the vacuum his passing left in all our lives.

The closing of the camps, in the fall of 1945, only aggravated what had begun inside. Papa had no money then and could not get work. Half of our family had already moved to the east coast, where jobs had opened up for them. The rest of us were relocated into a former defense workers' housing project in Long Beach. In that small apartment there never was enough room for all of us to sit down for a meal. We ate in shifts, and I yearned all the more for our huge round table in Ocean Park.

Soon after we were released I wrote a paper for a seventh-grade journalism class, describing how we used to hunt grunion before the war. The whole family would go down to Ocean Park Beach after dark, when the grunion were running, and build a big fire on the sand. I would watch Papa and my older brothers splash through the moonlit surf to scoop out the fish, then we'd rush back to the house where Mama would fry them up and set the sizzling pan on the table, with soy sauce and horseradish, for a midnight meal. I ended the paper with this sentence:

"The reason I want to remember this is because I know we'll never be able to do it again."

You might say it would have happened sooner or later anyway, this sliding apart of such a large family, in postwar California. People get married; their interests shift. But there is no escaping the fact that our internment accelerated the process, made it happen so suddenly it was almost tangible.

Not only did we stop eating at home, there was no longer a home to eat in. The cubicles we had were too small for anything you might call "living." Mama couldn't cook meals there. It was impossible to find any privacy there. We slept there and spent most of our waking hours elsewhere.

Mama had gone to work again soon after we arrived. The call went out for people with any kind of skill to offer their services. Thousands were responding, with great surges of community spirit, sometimes with outright patriotism, wanting "to do their part." Woody signed on as a carpenter. One of my brothers-in-law was a roofing foreman. Another ran a reservoir crew. Mama had worked as a dietician in Washington after she was married. In camp this was high-priority training. In addition to the daily multitude, those amateur cooks were faced with allergy cases, diabetics, nursing mothers, infants who required special feedings. For Mama it was also a way to make a little money. Nineteen dollars a month. This was top wage for an internee. Unskilled labor started at eight. All volunteer of course. You didn't have to get out of bed in the morning if you didn't want to. Mama wanted the work. She had a monthly fee to pay the warehouse in Los Angeles where she had stored what remained of our furniture and silver just before we evacuated. She worried about this constantly.

She worried about Papa too. Letters from him trickled in, once or twice a month, with half the words blacked out, calling her "Sweetheart" for the first time in fifteen years. She was always distracted, staring at things I could never see. I would try to get her attention, grab her around the legs. At night, in bed, she would hug me close. But during the day she never seemed to notice me.

Adrift, I began to look elsewhere for attention and thus took the first steps out of my child's realm toward a world of grownups other than my parents. Though I was only seven, my images of certain people from this period are very precise, because I had begun to *see* adults for the first time. On Terminal Island I first *saw* Orientals, those demon-children who had terrorized me. At Manzanar, past the fear of slanted eyes and high cheekbones, I watched with fresh amazement the variety of faces and bodies and costumes all around me. This may have resulted, in part, from the life Manzanar had forced upon us all. Once the weather warmed up, it was an out-of-doors life, where you only went "home" at night, when you finally had to: 10,000 people on an endless promenade inside the square mile of barbed wire that was the wall around our city.

One of our neighbors was a tall, broad woman, taller than anyone in camp, as far as I recall. She walked erectly and wore an Aunt Jemima scarf around her head. She was married to a Japanese man, and they had adopted a little Japanese girl I sometimes played with. But this woman, I realized much later, was half-black, with light mulatto skin, passing as a Japanese in order to remain with her husband. She wore scarves everywhere to cover her give-away hair.

In the barracks facing ours there lived an elegant

woman who astounded me each time I saw her. She and her husband both came from Japan, and her long aristocratic face was always a ghastly white. In traditional fashion she powdered it with rice flour every morning. By old-country standards this made her more beautiful. For a long time I thought she was diseased.

Two more white faces stand out in my memory, a pair of nurses I saw from time to time in the clinic. They wore white shoes, white hose, and white dresses. Above their bleached faces their foreheads had been shaved halfway over their scalp's curve to make a sharp widow's peak where starched black hair began to arch upward, reminding me of a cobra's hood. Their lips were gone. Their brows were plucked. They were always together, a pair of reptilian kabuki creatures at loose in the camp hospital.

You might say they were the negatives for two other women I soon began to see almost every day and, in fact, saw more of for a while than I did my mother. Their robes were black, their heads were hooded in white. Sister Mary Suzanne was about forty then, a frail, gentle woman from Japan who could speak no English. Sister Mary Bernadette was a feisty, robust little Canadian Japanese who spoke both languages fluently.

They were Maryknoll nuns, members of that missionary order whose special task is to go into a country, with knowledge of its language, and convert its people to the Catholic faith. Before the war they had run an orphanage in Los Angeles for children of Japanese ancestry. Evacuated to Manzanar and given the job of caring for some fifty orphans interned there, they set up what came to be known as "Children's Village," and they had one barracks turned into a chapel. They were joined by Father Steinback, one of the few Caucasians to live among us inside the compound and eat in our mess halls. He was greatly admired for this, and many internees converted to Catholicism before the camp was closed.

I was almost one of them. Papa stepped in just before my baptism day. If he had been there during those early months I probably would never have started spending time with the Maryknolls. He was always suspicious of organized religions. I think he had already tried to scare me away from Catholics. That was one of his prime methods of instruction: fear. On my way home from school each day in Ocean Park I would break into a run as I passed the local Catholic church. The nuns I glimpsed were robed and ghostly figures I wanted no part of.

Culturally we were like those Jews who observe certain traditions but never visit a synagogue. We kept a little Buddhist shrine in the house, and we celebrated a few Japanese holidays that were religiously connected—the way Christmas is. But we never said prayers. I had never been inside a Buddhist church. And as for Christianity, I had not heard the word God until we reached Terminal Island. I first heard about Jesus when the one friend I made there— another Japanese girl—took me to a Baptist Sunday School on the island, where a Caucasian teacher bewildered me with pictures of lambs and donkeys and golden-domed pavilions.

For some reason these did not appeal to me nearly as much as the stories of the saints and martyrs I heard a few months later when I began to study catechism with the Maryknolls. Soon I was over there every afternoon and most of Sunday. With no regular school to attend and no home to spend time in, it's no mystery that I should have been drawn to these two kind and generous women. They had organized a recreation program. They passed out candy. But what kept me coming back, once I started, were the tales of the unfortunate women like Saint Agatha, whose breasts were cut off when she refused to renounce her faith.

I had to walk nearly a mile to reach their chapel, and walk a mile back. That summer it was miserably hot, over one hundred degrees most days. Yet I made the trip gladly. A big homely girl about twenty years old who wore boys' shoes and an Eisenhower jacket taught catechism to the younger kids. She loved to sit us down and fix us with the eye of a mother superior and tell us about Saint Agatha, or Saint Juliana, who was boiled alive, or Saint Marcella, who was whipped to death by the Goths.

I was fascinated with the miseries of women who had suffered and borne such afflictions. On my way home, I would hike past row upon row of black barracks, watching mountains waver through that desert heat, with the sun trying to dry up my very blood, and imagine in some childish way that I was among them, that I too was up there on the screen of history, in a white lace catechism dress, sweating and grimy, yet selflessly carrying my load.

I fulfilled this little fantasy one blistering afternoon when the heat finally got me. Sunstroke. While crossing one of the wide sandy firebreaks that separated some of the blocks, I passed out.

This put me in bed for a week. After I recovered, several months went by before I resumed my catechism. For one thing, Papa discouraged me. It was just before this happened that he had returned from Fort Lincoln. He was back among us, making decisions, giving commands. For a while it seemed we would almost be a family again. But it didn't turn out that way. He was not the same man. Something terrible had happened to him in North Dakota.

He arrived at Manzanar on a Greyhound bus. We all went down to the main gate to meet him, everyone but Woody's wife, Chizu, who was in the camp hospital. The previous day she'd given birth to Papa's first grandson. She named him George, in honor of Papa's return. Two of my sisters were pregnant at the time, and they were there at the gate in hot-weather smocks, along with Woody, who had left the hospital long enough to welcome Papa back, and Granny and Mama and the rest of the family, a dozen of us standing in the glare, excited, yet very reverent as the bus pulled in.

The door whished open, and the first thing we saw was a cane—I will never forget it—poking from the shaded interior into sunlight, a straight, polished maple limb spotted with dark lidded eyes where small knotholes had been stained and polished.

Then Papa stepped out, wearing a fedora hat and a wilted white shirt. This was September 1942. He had been gone nine months. He had aged ten years. He looked over sixty, gaunt, wilted as his shirt, underweight, leaning on that cane and favoring his right leg. He stood there surveying his clan, and nobody moved, not even Mama, waiting to see what he would do or say, waiting for some cue from him as to how we should deal with this.

I was the only one who approached him. I had not thought of him much at all after he was taken away. He was simply gone. Now I was so happy to see him that I ran up and threw my arms around his waist and buried my face in his belt. I thought I should be laughing and welcoming him home. But I started to cry. By this time everyone was crying. No one else had moved yet to touch him. It was as if the youngest, the least experienced, had been appointed to display what the others, held back by awe or fear, or some old-country notion of respect for the patriarch, could not. I hugged him tighter, wanting to be happy that my father had come back. Yet I hurt so inside I could only welcome him with convulsive tears.

Chapter 6

Whatever He Did Had Flourish

That cane Papa brought back with him he had carved and polished himself in North Dakota. When his limp went away he continued to use it. He didn't need to. He liked it, as a kind of swagger stick, such as military officers sometimes use. When he was angry he would wield it like the flat of a sword, whacking out at his kids or his wife or his hallucinations. He kept that cane for years, and it served him well. I see it now as a sad, homemade version of the samurai sword his great-great-grandfather carried in the land around Hiroshima, at a time when such warriors weren't much needed anymore, when their swords were both their virtue and their burden. It helps me understand how Papa's life could end at a place like Manzanar. He didn't die there, but things finished for him there, whereas for me it was like a birthplace. The camp was where our life lines intersected.

He was the oldest son in a family that had for centuries been of the samurai class. He used to brag that they had owned more land than you could cross on horseback in a single day. By the time he was born, in 1887, they weren't warriors any longer. Japan was in the throes of that rapid, confusing metamorphosis from a feudal to an industrial nation, which began when Commodore Perry's black-hulled armada steamed into Tokyo Bay and forced the Japanese to open their ports and cities to western trade.

Papa's grandfather was a judge, at one point a magistrate for the small, lovely island of Miya-jima. He had four children, including one son, Papa's father. His three daughters were among the first women in Japan to receive university degrees. One daughter married an army general who for a time governed Formosa, and it was this uncle-general who encouraged Papa to enroll in a military school.

As far as everyone could see he was preparing for a career in the navy. Then, at seventeen, he abruptly dropped out. His favorite aunt lent him some money, and a short time later he bought passage on a ship bound for the Hawaiian Islands. That was the last anyone in Japan saw or heard of him.

In those days he was a headstrong idealist. He was spoiled, the ways eldest sons usually are in Japan, used to having his way, and he did not like what he saw happening to the family. Ironically, it foreshadowed just the sort of thing he himself would be faced with later on: too many children and not enough money. His father's first wife bore five children. When she died, he remarried and four more came along. His father, who had been a public official, ended up running a "teahouse" in Hiroshima— something like a cabaret. It was a living, but Papa wanted no part of this. In the traditional Japanese class system, samurai ranked just below nobility; then came farmers and those who worked the land. Merchants ranked fourth, below the farmers. For Papa, at seventeen, it made no difference that times were hard; the idea of a teahouse was an insult to the family name. What's more, their finances were in such a state that even as eldest son there was almost nothing for him to look forward to. The entire area around Hiroshima, mainly devoted to agriculture, was suffering a severe depression. In 1886 Japan had for the first time allowed its citizens to emigrate, and thousands from his district had already left the country in search of better opportunities. Papa followed them.

He reached Honolulu in 1904, with a letter of introduction to a cousin who taught school on Oahu. Papa used to tell the story of his first stroll through town, just off the boat and wanting to stretch his legs before looking up his relatives. He came across a sign outside a building that said in three languages Workers Wanted. Proud that he could read the English as well as the Japanese, he figured he'd have an edge over anyone else applying. He was feeling cocky anyway on this first day in the new world, seventeen years old and a little money burning in his pocket. He stepped into a men's shop a few doors down and bought himself a new suit, a new shirt, a new tie, a new hat—everything he'd seen the most prosperous men along the street wearing. He changed clothes in the store, then went to see about that job.

He followed arrows from the sign to the back of the building, where he found a yard full of half-dressed Chinese and Japanese field hands waiting in line to apply for work in the sugar cane. His disdain for them was met with laughter. They looked at him as if he were a maniac, pointing with derision at his dandy's outfit. He rushed back to the street, cursing, dismayed, humiliated, heading for the safety of his cousin's.

A few weeks later he was introduced to a vacationing American, a lawyer from Idaho who offered to pay his passage to the states and provide room and board in exchange for three years' work as a houseboy. Papa accepted. It looked better than sweating in the fields, which was how most of his countrymen were making their new start. And one imagines that the American mainland glittered for him the way it did for all those entrepreneurs and pilgrims and runaways and adventurers who crossed the Atlantic and the Pacific hoping to carve out a piece of it for themselves.

In Idaho he worked as a valet, a cook, a chauffeur, a mechanic, a general handyman. He learned to roast turkeys and to drive a Pierce-Arrow sedan, and he perfected the English he had begun to learn before he left Japan.

In all, he spent five years with this family. Then his patron helped him enter the University of Idaho as an undergraduate, aiming toward a law degree. Papa used to joke that if he hadn't met Mama he might have ended up a senator.

"She was too pretty," her brother Charlie once said. "Ko couldn't leave her alone. She was the only Japanese girl in the whole northwest worth looking at. I think there were two others around in those days, and they were both so skinny they could hide behind cornstalks."

Mama's father came from a family of stonecutters around Niigata, on the inner coast of northern Japan. But she was born in Hawaii where her father had come to do the backbreaking work Papa luckily avoided—a three-year labor contract on a sugar-cane plantation, ten hours a day, six days a week, for twelve dollars and fifty cents a month. Completing that, he worked his way to the mainland and set out with his three sons to find a piece of land. They settled in the rich farm country around Spokane, in eastern Washington. In 1906 Mama and Granny joined them there. Granny was thirty then, Mama was ten. They sailed into San Francisco Bay on the morning after the earthquake and spent their first three days in America sitting offshore watching the city go up in flames.

Her family had high hopes for Mama. She was their only daughter. In those days Japanese women on the mainland were rare, one for every seven or eight Japanese men. Most men had to go back to Japan to find a woman, or take their chances on a "picture bride." Mama was worth a lot, and before she finished high school they had promised her to the upright son of a well-to-do farmer in the territory.

She met Papa early one summer morning at a wholesale market where her family sold produce. Papa was unloading trucks and wagonloads of vegetables. She was seventeen, small, buxom, with a classically round face of a kind much admired among Japanese. He was twenty-five, a sometime law student who spent his summers working around Spokane. He liked to shoot pool in his spare time, he played cards and dressed like a man from a much flashier part of the country. He was also pitching for a semipro baseball team called *Nippon*. We have a picture of him down on one knee for the team photo, in the front row, his mitted left hand resting on the other knee, his thick hair loose, his eyes showing a cocky confidence. His lean jaw bulges slightly, as if holding a small plug of tobacco, in the manner of Ty Cobb, whose style was the one to imitate about that time.

Mama's parents were terrified when they saw him coming. He not only led what seemed to them a perilously fast life; he also borrowed money. The story goes that he once asked Mama to borrow as much as she could from Granny. All Granny had at the time was a five-dollar bill. She gave it to Mama, who passed it on to Papa, who then came stalking into the kitchen, stiff-backed, glaring scornfully at Granny. He was insulted. "It's not enough," he said. "Five dollars. I need more than five dollars. If that's all you've got, I'd rather have nothing!" And he threw the bill into the fire.

The first time Mama ran away with him, her brothers came looking for her, brought her back to the family farm, and locked her in a second-story room. Mama was so desolate, her oldest brother Charlie couldn't stand it. He leaned a ladder up to her window, forced the latch and let her out.

That time they got away, got married, and made it down to Salem, Oregon, where Papa cooked in a restaurant and she worked as a nurse and dietician until my oldest brother was born, in 1916.

After that she had a child about every two years, nine in the next eighteen, and Papa kept moving, looking for the job, or the piece of land, or the inspiration that would make him his fortune and give him the news he hoped all his life he would one day be able to send back to his relatives: *Wakatsuki Ko made it big in America and has restored some honor to his family's name.*

Education mattered a great deal to him. In later years he would brag to us that he "went to law school" and imply that he held some kind of degree from a northern university. It's true that everywhere he stopped he'd be helping a friend through one legal squabble or another—an immigration problem, a repossessed fishing boat. He worked for the government at one point, translating legal documents. But as badly as he wanted us to believe it, he never did finish law school. Who knows why? He was terribly proud, sometimes absurdly proud, and he refused to defer to any man. Maybe, in training for that profession in those years before the First World War, he saw ahead of him prejudices he refused to swallow, humiliations he refused to bear.

On the other hand, his schooling was like almost everything else he tried. For all his boasts and high intentions, he never quite finished anything he set out to do. Something always stopped him: bad luck, a racial barrier, a law, his own vanity or arrogance or fear of losing face.

For a couple of years he tried lumberjacking in Seattle. We have another old photo, this one from the twenties, that shows him standing on a railroad siding, with his boots spread wide, one hand in his jeans pocket and the other holding a wide-brim hat flung high in boisterous greeting—a Nipponese frontiersman with the pine forests rising behind him.

In Oregon he learned a little dentistry (a skill he later put to good used at Manzanar, where he made dozens of dentures free of charge). He tried farming there too. The alien land laws prevented him from owning property, but he could lease the land, or make a tenancy deal and work it.

A few years before I was born he had settled the family on a twenty-two-acre farm near Watsonville, California, raising apples, strawberries, and a few vegetable crops. He was making good money, living in a big Victorian house, and it looked as if he'd found his castle at last. But his luck didn't hold. The well went dry. Thirty years after sailing away from a financial dead end and the remnants of a once-noble family in Japan, he found himself in the middle of America's Depression and on the move again, with eight kids and a wife this time, working his way down the California coast picking prunes, peaches, Brussels sprouts, sending his children into the orchards like any migrant worker's family, hoping their combined earnings would leave a little left over after everyone was fed and the cars gassed up for the next day's search for work.

Just before I was born he leased another piece of land, in Inglewood, outside Los Angeles, and farmed again, briefly. Then, deciding land was too risky for investing either time or money, he turned to the ocean, started fishing out of Santa Monica, and did well enough at it through the late thirties that by December of 1941 he had those two boats, *The Waka* and *The Nereid,* a lease on that beach house in Ocean Park, and a nearly new Studebaker he had made a down payment on two weeks before Pearl Harbor was attacked.

The start of World War II was not the climax to our life in Ocean Park. Pearl Harbor just snipped it off, stopped it from becoming whatever else lay ahead. Papa might have lost his business anyway—who knows—sunk his boat perhaps, the way Woody almost sank one off Santa Monica a few years later, when he motored into the largest school of mackerel he'd ever seen, got so excited hauling in the fish he let them pile up on deck, and didn't notice water slipping through the gunwale slits and into the hold until the bow went under.

If any single event climaxed those prewar years, it was, for me at least, the silver wedding anniversary we celebrated in 1940. Papa was elegant that day, in a brand-new double-breasted worsted suit, with vest and silk tie and stickpin. He was still the dude, always the dude, no matter what, spending more money on his clothes than on anything else. Mama wore a long, crocheted, rose-colored dress. And I see them standing by our round dining room table, this time heaped not with food but with silver gifts—flatware, tureens, platters, trays, gravy bowls, and brandy snifters. The food was spread along a much larger table, buffet style, in glistening abundance—chicken teriyaki, pickled vegetables, egg rolls, cucumber and abalone salad, the seaweed-wrapped rice balls called *sushi,* shrimp, prawns, fresh lobster, and finally, taking up what seemed like half the tablecloth, a great gleaming roast pig with a bright red apple in its mouth.

A lot of in-laws were there, and other Japanese families, and Papa's fishing cronies, a big Portuguese named Goosey who used to eat small hot yellow peppers in one big bite, just to make me laugh, and an Italian named Blackie, with long black sideburns and black hair slicked straight back, wearing black and white shoes and a black suit with white pinstripes. These two were his drinking buddies, as flushed now as Papa was from the hot sake that was circulating and the beer and whiskey.

Papa announced that it was time to carve the pig. We all stood back to make a wide half circle around that end of the table. He had supervised the roasting, now he was going to show us how you cut up a pig. When he knew everyone was watching this—we were his audience, this dining room his theater—he lifted a huge butcher's cleaver, and while Goosey and Blackie, trying not to giggle, held each side of a long cutting board beneath its neck, Papa chopped the head off in two swift, crunching strokes. All the men cheered—the sons, the carousers. The women sucked in their breath and murmured. Three more strokes and Papa had the animal split—two sides of roast pork steaming from within. With serious face and a high-held, final flick he split each side in half, quartering the pig. Then he set the cleaver down, stepped back, reached behind him without looking for a towel one of my sisters somehow had there waiting, and as he wiped his hands he said imperiously to his sons, "Cut it up. You girls, bring the platters here. Everybody wants to eat."

That's how I remember him before he disappeared. He was not a great man. He wasn't even a very successful man. He was a poser, a braggart, and a tyrant. But he had held onto his self-respect, he dreamed grand dreams, and he could work well at any task he turned his hand to: he could raise vegetables, sail a boat, plead a case in small claims court, sing Japanese poems, make false teeth, carve a pig.

Whatever he did had flourish. Men who knew him at Fort Lincoln remember him well. They were all Issei, and he was one of the few fluent in Japanese and English. Each morning the men would gather in their common room and he would read the news aloud, making a performance of it by holding the American paper in front of him and translating into Japanese on the spot, orating the news, altering his voice to suit the senator, the general, or the movie star.

Papa worked as an interviewer there, helping the Justice Department interview other Isseis. He almost became an alcoholic there on rice wine the men learned to brew in the barracks. And somehow, during the winter of '42, both of his feet were frostbitten. No one quite knows how. Papa never talked about that to anyone after he got back. But it isn't difficult to imagine. He arrived from Long Beach, California, at the beginning of January, in a country where cattle often freeze to death, and he was of course a prisoner of war.

Chapter 7

Fort Lincoln: An Interview

"What is your full name?"

"Wakatsuki Ko."

"Your place of birth?"

"Ka-ke, a small town in Hiroshima-ken, on the island of Honshu."

"What schools did you attend in Japan?"

"Four years in Chuo Gakko, a school for training military officers."

"Why did you leave?"

"The marching. I got tired of the marching. That was not what I wanted to do."

"Have you any relatives serving in the military, now or in the past?"

"My uncle was a general, a rather famous general. He led the regiment which defeated the Russians at Port Arthur in nineteen five."

"Have you ever been in contact with him since coming to the United States?"

"No. I have contacted no one in Japan."

"Why not?"

"I am what you call the black sheep in the family."

"So you have never returned to your homeland?"

"No."

"Because you are the black sheep."

"And because I have never been able to afford the trip. I have ten children."

"What are their names?"

"How can I remember that many names?"

"Try."

"William is the oldest. Then Eleanor, Woodrow, Frances, Lillian, Reijiro, Martha, Kiyo, and let's see, yes, May."

"That is only nine."

"Nine?"

"You said there were ten."

"I told you, it is too many to remember."

"It says here that you are charged with delivering oil to Japanese submarines off the coast of California."

"That is not true."

"Several submarines have been sighted there."

"If I had seen one, I would have laughed."

"Why?"

"Only a very foolish commander would take such a vessel that far from his home fleet."

"How can you explain this photograph?"

"Let me see it."

"Aren't those two fifty-gallon drums on the deck of your boat?"

"Yes."

"What were you carrying in fifty-gallon drums ten miles from shore?"

"Chum."

"Chum?"

"Bait. Fish guts. Ground-up fish heads. You dump it overboard and it draws the mackerel, and you pull in your nets, and they are full of fresh fish. Who took this photograph anyway? I haven't gone after

mackerel in over a year."

"What do you think of the attack on Pearl Harbor?"

"I am sad for both countries. It is the kind of thing that always happens when military men are in control."

"What do you think of the American military? Would you object to your sons serving?"

"Yes. I would protest it. The American military is just like the Japanese."

"What do you mean?"

"They also want to make war when it is not necessary. As long as military men control the country you are always going to have a war."

"Who do you think will win this one?"

"America, of course. It is richer, has more resources, more weapons, more people. The Japanese are courageous fighters, and they will fight well. But their leaders are stupid. I weep every night for my country."

"You say Japan is still your country?"

"I was born there. I have relatives living there. In many ways, yes, it is still my country."

"Do you feel any loyalty to Japan or to its Emperor?"

Silence.

"I said, do you feel any loyalty . . ."

"How old are you?"

"Twenty-nine."

"When were you born?"

"I am the interrogator here, Mr. Wakatsuki, not you."

"I am interested to know when you were born."

"Nineteen thirteen."

"I have been living in this country nine years longer than you have. Do you realize that? Yet I am prevented by law from becoming a citizen. I am

prevented by law from owning land. I am now separated from my family without cause . . ."

"Those matters are out of my hands, Mr. Wakatsuki."

"Whose hands are they in?"

"I do not like North Dakota any more than you do. The sooner we finish these questions, the sooner we'll both be out of here."

"And where will you go when you leave?"

"Who do you want to win this war?"

"I am interested to know where you will be going when you leave."

"Mr. Wakatsuki, if I have to repeat each one of these questions we will be here forever. Who do you want . . . ?"

"When your mother and your father are having a fight, do you want them to kill each other? Or do you just want them to stop fighting?"

Chapter 8

Inu

With Papa back our cubicle was filled to overflowing. Woody brought in another army bunk and tick mattress, up next to Mama's. But that was not what crowded the room. It was Papa himself, his dark, bitter, brooding presence. Once moved in, it seemed he didn't go outside for months. He sat in there, or paced, alone a great deal of the time, and Mama had to bring his meals from the mess hall.

He made her bring him extra portions of rice, or cans of the syrupy fruit they served. He would save this up and concoct brews in a homemade still he kept behind the door, brews that smelled so bad Mama was ashamed to let in any visitors. Day after day he would sip his rice wine or his apricot brandy, sip till he was blind drunk and passed out. In the morning he would wake up groaning like the demon in a kabuki drama; he would vomit and then start sipping again. He terrified all of us, lurching around the tiny room, cursing in Japanese and swinging his bottles wildly. No one could pacify him. Mama got nothing but threats and abuse for her attempts to comfort him.

I turned eight that fall. I remember telling myself that he never went out and never associated with others because he thought he was better than they were and was angry at being forced to live so close to them for the first time in his life. I told myself they whispered about him because he brewed his own foul-smelling wine in our barracks.

All of this was partly true. But there were deeper, uglier reasons for his isolation. I first sensed it one night when Mama and I went to the latrine together. By this time the stalls were partitioned. Two Terminal Island women about Mama's age were leaving just as we walked in. They lingered by the doorway, and from inside my stall I could hear them whispering about Papa, deliberately, just loud enough for us to hear. They kept using the word "inu." I knew it meant "dog," and I thought at the time they were backbiting him because he never socialized.

Spoken Japanese is full of disrespectful insult words that can be much more cutting than mere vulgarity. They have to do with bad manners, or worse, breaches of faith and loyalty. Years later I learned that *inu* also meant collaborator or informer. Members of the Japanese American Citizens League were being called *inu* for having helped the army arrange a peaceful and orderly evacuation. Men who cooperated with camp authorities in any way could be labeled *inu,* as well as those genuine informers inside the camp who relayed information to the War Department and to the FBI.

For the women in the late-night latrine Papa was an *inu* because he had been released from Fort Lincoln earlier than most of the Issei men, many of whom had to remain up there separated from their families throughout the war. After investigating his record, the Justice Department found no reason to detain him any longer. But the rumor was that, as an interpreter, he had access to information from fellow Isseis that he later used to buy his release.

This whispered charge, added to the shame of everything that had happened to him, was simply more than he could bear. He did not yet have the strength to resist it. He exiled himself, like a leper, and he drank.

The night Mama and I came back from the latrine with this newest bit of gossip, he had been drinking all day. At the first mention of what we'd overheard, he flew into a rage. He began to curse her for listening to such lies, then he cursed her for leaving him alone and wanted to know where she had *really* gone. He cursed her for coming back and disturbing him, for not bringing him his food on time, for bringing too much cabbage and not enough rice. He yelled and shook his fists and with his very threats forced her across the cluttered room until she collided with one of the steel bed frames and fell back onto a mattress.

I had crawled under another bunk and huddled, too frightened to cry. In a house I would have run to another room, but in the tight little world of our cubicle there was no escaping this scene. I knew his wrath could turn on any one of us. Kiyo was already in bed, scrunched down under the covers, hoping not to be seen. Mama began to weep, great silent tears, and Papa was now limping back and forth beside the bunk, like a caged animal, brandishing his long, polished North Dakota cane.

"I'm going to kill you this time!"

"Go ahead, if that will make you happy."

"You lie to me. You imprison me here with your lies!"

"Kill me then. I don't care. I just don't care."

"I can never go outside, because of you!"

"Here. Here is my head. My chest. Get it over with.

Who wants to go on living like this?"

She was lying very still, gazing up at him. The tears had stopped.

Papa stood over her, gripping his cane in both hands, right above her head, holding it so tightly the cane and both his arms quivered. "All right!" he yelled. "All right, I will! I will! I will!"

We had watched many scenes like this since his return, with Papa acting so crazy sometimes you could almost laugh at the samurai in him, trying to cow her with sheer noise and fierce display. But these were still unfamiliar visits from a demon we had never seen when we lived in Ocean Park. There had always been doors to keep some moments private. Here there were no doors. Nothing was private. And tonight he was far too serious—he seemed to have reached some final limit.

Inside my own helplessness I cowered, sure he was going to kill her or hurt her very badly, and the way Mama lay there I believed she was actually ready to be beaten to death. Kiyo must have felt something similar, because at the height of Papa's tirade he threw his covers back, and in his underwear he jumped out of bed yelling, "Stop it, Papa! Stop it!"

With his cane in both hands high above his head, Papa turned from the waist. Kiyo sprang across the room, one arm cocked, and punched Papa square in the face.

No one had ever seen such a thing before. Papa's arms went limp. The cane fell clattering to the floor. He reached up and touched his nose. Blood was pouring onto his shirt, dripping down onto Mama's dress. Kiyo stepped back, crouching, staring at the blood. This was like bloodying the nose of God. His face, contorted, looked ready to cry, but even his tears were stopped by the knowledge of what he had done.

He waited paralyzed for whatever punishment might strike him down. Papa couldn't move either. He stared at Kiyo, his eyes wide with both outrage and admiration that his son had the courage to do this. They stood like that until Papa's gaze went bleary from the drink in his veins and dropped to the damp shirt, to the blood still spattering onto Mama's dress.

Kiyo turned and bolted out the door. I ran over to Mama, whimpering with relief that this ghastly scene was over and she had been saved, yet aching with a great sadness I could not at the time find words for. I was proud of Kiyo and afraid for what would happen to him; but deeper than that, I felt the miserable sense of loss that comes when the center has collapsed and everything seems to be flying apart around you.

Kiyo had fled to one of my married sisters' barracks. For two weeks he hid there. When he finally returned it was to admit that he had been in the wrong and to ask Papa's forgiveness. He too wanted some order preserved in the world and in the family. Papa accepted his apology, and this settled the waters some. But that aching sadness did not go away. It was something undefinable I'd already been living with for months, now enflamed by Papa's downfall. He kept pursuing oblivion through drink, he kept abusing Mama, and there seemed to be no way out of it for anyone. You couldn't even run.

Chapter 9

The Mess Hall Bells

Papa never said more than three or four sentences about his nine months at Fort Lincoln. Few men who spent time there will talk about it more than that. Not because of the physical hardships: he had been through worse times on fishing trips down the coast of Mexico. It was the charge of disloyalty. For a man raised in Japan, there was no greater disgrace. And it was the humiliation. It brought him face to face with his own vulnerability, his own powerlessness. He had no rights, no home, no control over his own life. This kind of emasculation was suffered, in one form or another, by all the men interned at Manzanar. Papa's was an extreme case. Some coped with it better than he, some worse. Some retreated. Some struck back.

During that first summer and fall of sandy congestion and wind-blown boredom, the bitterness accumulated, the rage festered in hundreds of tarpapered cubicles like ours. Looking back, what they now call the December Riot seems to have been inevitable. It happened exactly a year after the Pearl Harbor attack. Some have called this an anniversary demonstration organized by militantly pro-Japan forces in the camp. It wasn't as simple as that. Everything just came boiling up at once.

In the months before the riot the bells rang often at our mess hall, sending out the calls for public meetings. They rang for higher wages, they rang for better food, they rang for open revolt, for patriotism, for common sense, and for a wholesale return to Japan. Some meetings turned into shouting sessions. Some led to beatings. One group tried to burn down the general store. Assassination threats were commonplace.

On the night of December 5, Fred Tayama, a leader in the Japanese American Citizens League and a "friend" of the administration, was badly beaten by six men and taken to the camp hospital for treatment. Tayama couldn't identify anyone precisely, but the next day three men were arrested and one of these was sent out of the camp to the country jail at Independence, ten miles away. This was a young cook well known for his defiance and contempt for the authorities. He had been trying to organize a Kitchen Workers' Union and had recently charged the camp's chief steward, a Caucasian, with stealing sugar and meat from the warehouses to sell on the black market. Since sugar and meat were both in short supply, and since it was rumored that infants had died from saccharin mixed into formulas as a sugar substitute, these charges were widely believed. The young cook's arrest became the immediate and popular cause that triggered the riot.

I was too young to witness any of it. Papa himself did not take part and he kept all of us with him in the barracks during the day and night it lasted. But I remember the deadly quiet in the camp the morning before it began, that heavy atmospheric threat of something about to burst. And I remember hearing the crowds rush past our block that night. Toward the end of if they were a lynch mob, swarming from one side of the camp to the other, from the hospital to the police station to the barracks of the men they were after, shouting slogans in English and Japanese.

"Idiots," Papa called them. "*Bakatare*. They want to go back to Japan."

"It is more than going back to Japan," Mama said. "It is the sugar. It disappears so fast . . ."

"What do they think they will find over there?"

"Maybe they would be treated like human beings," Mama said.

"You be quiet. Listen to what I am saying. These idiots won't even get to the front gate of this camp. You watch. Before this is over, somebody is going to be killed. I guarantee it. They might all be killed."

The man who emerged as leader of the rioters was Hawaiian-born Joe Kurihara. During the First World War he had served in the U.S. Army in France and in Germany, and he was so frustrated by his treatment at Manzanar he was ready to renounce his citizenship and sail to the old country. Kurihara's group set up microphones and speakers near the cook's barracks and began a round of crowd-stirring speeches, demanding his release, charging that Tayama and the administration had used this beating to cover up the sugar fraud and saying it was time to get the *inus* once and for all.

That afternoon the authorities agreed to bring the young cook back into camp. But this wasn't enough. By 6:00 P.M. 2,000 people were looking for blood. The Internal Security Force, made up of internees like the demonstrators, had evaporated in the face of such a mob. For a while they had the camp to themselves.

They split into two groups, one heading for the

police station to free the cook, the other heading for the hospital to finish off Tayama, who had been concealed under a hospital bed. A vigilante party searched the corridors. When they failed to find their man, this half of the crowd moved off in search of others on their "death list."

Meanwhile the mob heading for the police station had been met by a detachment of military police carrying submachine guns and M-1s. When an army captain asked them to disperse, they stoned him. Now they were hooting "*Banzai!*," jeering threats at the MPs and singing songs in Japanese. The MPs started lobbing tear gas bombs, and then, with no announcement or command to shoot, while the mob swirled frantically to escape the gas, several soldiers opened fire.

This instantly cleared the street, and the riot was over. Only the dead and the injured remained. Ten were treated in the hospital for gunshot wounds. One young man was killed on the spot. Another nineteen-year-old died five days later.

What I recall vividly are the bells that began to toll late that night. After dispersing, some of the demonstrators organized shifts, and kept them tolling all over camp. With the bells and the MP jeeps patrolling up and down the streets, I was a long time getting to sleep. Against Papa's orders I kept sneaking looks out the window, and I saw something I had only seen once before. The searchlights. They operated every night, but I never saw them because I went to bed so early and our block was well in from the perimeter. From the guard towers the lights scanned steadily, making shadows ebb and flow among the barracks like dark, square waves.

The next morning I awoke long after sunup. The lights were gone. Shadows were sharp and fixed. But the bells were still ringing. It was the only sound in camp, the only sound in Owens Valley, the mess hall bells, their gongs echoing between the Inyo Range and the nearby Sierras, their furthest ripples soaking into dry sand. They rang till noon.

Chapter 10

The Reservoir Shack:
An Aside

My brother-in-law Kaz was foreman of a reservoir maintenance detail, the only crew permitted to work or to leave the camp limits the night of the riot. At the back gate they were issued four pickax handles, to protect themselves in case the inu-hunters found them "cooperating" at a time like this.

They drove out there, checked the chlorine shed, toured the perimeter, then trooped into a little shack that had been set up with four cots. It was like a fireman's watch. Each crew spent twenty-four hours on standby, making periodic checks, clearing the debris, doing whatever was necessary to keep the water moving into camp.

The shack had one window, but when they turned off the light and stretched out on the cots, you could barely see its outline, the night was so dark. Kaz lay there trying to see the line between the dark inside and the dark outside the shack, and he thought he saw something pass across the window but called it his imagination and shut his eyes.

A moment later the door crashed open. A flashlight was blinding him. He felt the sharp jut of a gunsight against his cheek.

Someone yelled, "All right, you Japs, up against the wall!"

He jumped out of bed and saw four MPs with Tommy guns, a sergeant and three privates. While Kaz backed to the wall to join his crew, that gun barrel stayed right against his cheek. The MPs kept yelling, "C'mon Japs, move it. Move it!"

Kaz finally found his voice. "Hey! What's the matter with you guys?"

The sergeant in charge was wild-eyed, scanning the room as he fanned the air with his Tommy gun, sure he had uncovered a nest of saboteurs. He was about the same age as Kaz, early twenties.

"What the hell are you doing out here?" he yelled.

"We're the reservoir crew."

"Nobody's supposed to leave the camp! You know that!"

"Somebody's gotta be out here all the time. Regulations."

The sergeant spotted the ax handles on the floor by each cot and kicked one with his boot.

"What the hell are these for then?"

"The rioters. If they found us here they'd throw us all in the reservoir."

The sergeant squinted suspiciously.

Kaz said, "Go on back to the gate and check it out."

The sergeant kicked all the ax handles into a pile and scooped them up. "I'm taking these with me. Don't nobody move till I get back."

He left. The reservoir crew didn't blink until he returned with the clearance half an hour later. They stood there watching the three jittery privates, who *had backed up against the opposite wall, as fearful as these four Japs they had to guard as Kaz and his men were of the unsteady weapons they knew could go off at any moment.*

Chapter 11

Yes Yes No No

27. Are you willing to serve in the Armed Forces of the United States on combat duty, wherever ordered?

<u>   </u>   <u>   </u>

(yes)   (no)

28. Will you swear unqualified allegiance to the United States of America and faithfully defend the United States from any or all attack by foreign or domestic forces, and forswear any form of allegiance or obedience to the Japanese emperor, or any other foreign government, power, or organization?

<u>   </u>   <u>   </u>

(yes)   (no)

—from the *War Relocation Authority Application for Leave Clearance, 1943*

Later in December the administration gave each family a Christmas tree hauled in from the Sierras. A new director had been appointed and this was his gesture of apology for all the difficulties that had led up to the riot, a promise of better treatment and better times to come.

It was an honest gesture, but it wasn't much of a Christmas that year. The presents were makeshift, the wind was roaring, Papa was drunk. Better times were a long way off, and the difficulties, it seemed, had just begun. Early in February the government's Loyalty Oath appeared. Everyone seventeen and over was required to fill it out. This soon became the most divisive issue of all. It cut deeper than the riot, because no one could avoid it. Not even Papa. After five months of self-imposed isolation, this debate was what finally forced him out of the barracks and into circulation again.

At the time, I was too young to understand the problem. I only knew there was no peace in our cubicle for weeks. Block organizers would come to talk to Papa and my brothers. They would huddle over the table awhile, muttering like conspirators, sipping tea or one of his concoctions. Their voices gradually would rise to shouts and threats. Mama would try to calm the men down. Papa would tell her to shut up, then Granny would interrupt and order him to quit disgracing Mama all the time. Once he just shoved Granny across the room, up against the far wall and back into her chair, and where she sat sniffling while the arguments went on.

If the organizers weren't there, Papa would argue with Woody. Or rather, Woody would listen to Papa lecture him on *true* loyalty, pacing from bunk to bunk, waving his cane.

"Listen to me, Woodrow. When a soldier goes into war he must go believing he is never coming back. This is why the Japanese are such courageous warriors. They are prepared to die. They expect nothing else. But to do that, you must *believe* in what you're fighting for. If you do not believe, you will not be willing to die. If you are not willing to die, you won't fight well. And if you don't fight well you will probably be killed stupidly, for the wrong reason, and unheroically. So tell me, how can you think of going off to fight?"

Woody always answered softly, respectfully, with a boyish and submissive smile.

"I will fight well, Papa."

"In this war? How is it possible?"

"I am an American citizen. America is at war."

"But look where they have put us!"

"The more of us who go into the army, the sooner the war will be over, the sooner you and Mama will be out of here."

"Do you think I would risk losing a son for that?"

"You want me to answer NO NO, Papa?"

"Do you think that is what I'm telling you? Of course you cannot answer NO NO. If you say NO NO, you will be shipped back to Japan with all those other *bakatare!*"

"But if I answer YES YES I will be drafted anyway, no matter how I feel about it. That is why they are giving us the oath to sign."

"No! That is not true! They are looking for volunteers. And only a fool would volunteer."

Papa stared hard at Woody, making this a challenge. Woody shrugged, still smiling his boyish smile, and did not argue. He knew that when the time came he would join the army, and he knew it was pointless to begin the argument again. It was a circle. His duty as a son was to sit and listen to Papa thrash his way around it and around it and around it.

A circle, or you might have called it a corral, like Manzanar itself, with no exit save via three narrow gates. The first led into the infantry, the second back across the Pacific. The third, called *relocation,* was just opening up: interned citizens who could find a job and a sponsor somewhere inland, away from the west coast, were beginning to trickle out of camp. But the program was bogged down in paperwork. It was taking months to process applications and security clearances. A loyalty statement required of everyone, it was hoped, might save some time and a lot of red tape. This, together with the search for "loyal" soldiers, had given rise to the ill-fated "oath."

Two weeks before the December Riot, JACL leaders met in Salt Lake City and passed a resolution pledging Nisei to volunteer out of the camps for military service.* In January the government announced its plan to form an all-Nisei combat regiment. While recruiting for this unit and speeding up the relocation program, the government figured it could simultaneously weed out the "disloyal" and thus get a clearer idea of exactly how many agents and Japanese sympathizers it actually had to deal with. This part of it would have been comical if the results were not so grotesque. No self-respecting espionage agent would willingly admit he was disloyal. Yet the very idea of the oath itself—appearing at the end of that first chaotic year—became the final goad that

---

* At the time this move was widely condemned, and *inu* charges escalated. That was, in fact, one of the causes for Tayama's beating. Since then history has proved the JACL was right. Mike Masaoka, who pushed the resolution through, understood that the most effective way Japanese Americans could combat the attitudes that put them in places like Manzanar was to shed their blood on the battlefield. The all-Nisei 442nd Regimental Combat Team was the most decorated American unit in World War II; it also suffered the highest percentage of casualties and deaths. They were much admired, and the JACL strategy succeeded. This was visible *proof* that these 110,000 people could be trusted.

prodded many once-loyal citizens to turn militantly anti-American.

From the beginning Papa knew his own answer would be YES YES. He agreed with Woody on this much, even though it meant swearing allegiance to the government that had sent him to Fort Lincoln and denying his connections with the one country in the world where he might still have the rights of a citizen. The alternative was worse. If he said NO NO, he could be sent to Tule Lake camp in northern California where all the "disloyal" were to be assembled for what most people believed would be eventual repatriation to Japan. Papa had no reason to return to Japan. He was too old to start over. He believed America would win the war, and he knew, even after all he'd endured, that if he had a future it still lay in this country. What's more, a move to Tule Lake could mean a further splitting up of our family.

This was a hard choice to make, and even harder to hold to. Anti-American feeling in camp ran stronger than ever. Pro-Japan forces were trying to organize a NO NO vote by blocks, in massive resistance. Others wanted to boycott the oath altogether in a show of noncooperation or through the mistaken fear that *anyone* who accepted the form would be shipped out of camp: the NO NOs back to Japan, the YES YESes into an American society full of wartime hostility and racial hate.

A meeting to debate the matter was called in our mess hall. Papa knew that merely showing his face would draw stares and muttered comments. YES YES was just what they expected of an *inu*. But he had to speak his mind before the NO NO contingent carried the block. Saying NO NO as an individual was one thing, bullying the entire camp into it was quite another. At the very least he didn't want to be sucked into such a decision without having his own opinion heard.

Woody wanted to go with him, but Papa said it was a meeting for "heads of households" only and he insisted on going alone. From the time he heard about it he purposely drank nothing stronger than tea. He shaved and trimmed his mustache and put on a silk tie. His limp was nearly gone now, but he carried his cane and went swaggering off down the narrow walkway between the barracks, punching at the packed earth in front of him.

About four o'clock I was playing hopscotch in the firebreak with three other girls. It was winter, the sun had already dropped behind Mount Whitney. Now a wind was rising, the kind of biting, steady wind that could bring an ocean of sand into camp at any moment with almost no warning. I was hurrying back to the barracks when I heard a great commotion inside the mess hall, men shouting wildly, as if a fire had broken out. The loudest voice was Papa's, cursing.

"*Eta!* (trash) *Eta! Bakayaro! Bakayaro!*"

The door of the mess hall flew open and a short, beefy man came tearing out. He jumped off the porch, running as his feet hit the ground. He didn't get far. Papa came through the doorway right behind him, in a flying leap, bellowing like a warrior, "Yaaaaaah!" He let go of his cane as he landed on the man's back, and they both tumbled into the dirt. The wind was rising. Half the sky was dark with a tide of sand pouring toward us. The dust billowed and spun as they kicked and pummeled and thrashed each other.

At the meeting, when Papa stood up to defend the YES YES position, murmurs of "*Inu, inu*" began to circulate around the mess hall. This man then jumped up at the speaker's table and made the charge aloud. Papa went for him. Now, outside in the dirt, Papa had him by the throat and would have strangled him, but some other men pulled them apart. I had never seen him so livid, yelling and out of his head with rage. While they pinned his arms, he kicked at the sand, sending windblown bursts of it toward the knot of men dragging his opponent out of reach.

A few moments later the sandstorm hit. The sky turned black as night. Everyone ran for cover. Two men hustled Papa to our barracks. The fighting against the wind and sand to get there calmed him down some.

Back inside he sat by the stove holding his teacup and didn't speak for a long time. One cheekbone was raw where it had been mashed into the sand. Mama kept pouring him little trickles of tea. We listened to the wind howl. When the sand died down, the sky outside stayed black. The storm had knocked out the electricity all over the camp. It was a cold, lonely night, and we huddled around our oil stove while Mama and Woody and Chizu began to talk about the day.

A young woman came in, a friend of Chizu's, who lived across the way. She had studied in Japan for several years. About the time I went to bed she and Papa began to sing songs in Japanese, warming their hands on either side of the stove, facing each other in its glow. After a while Papa sang the first line of the Japanese national anthem, *Kimi ga yo*. Woody, Chizu, and Mama knew the tune, so they hummed along while Papa and the other woman sang the words. It can be a hearty or a plaintive tune, depending on your mood. From Papa, that night, it was a deep-throated lament. Almost invisible in the stove's small glow, tears began running down his face.

I had seen him cry a few times before. It only happened when he was singing or when someone else sang a song that moved him. He played the three-stringed *samisen*, which Kiyo and I called his "pinko-pinko." We would laugh together when we heard him plucking it and whining out old Japanese melodies. We would hold our ears and giggle. It was always a great joke between us, except for those rare times when Papa began to weep at the lyrics. Then we would just stare quietly—as I did that night—from some hidden corner of the room. This was always mysterious and incomprehensible.

The national anthem, I later learned, is what he had sung every morning as a schoolboy in Japan. They still sing it there, the way American kids pledge allegiance to the flag. It is not a martial song, or a victory song, the way many national anthems are. It is really a poem, whose words go back to the ninth century:

> *Kimi ga yo wa chiyoni*
> *yachiyoni sa-za-re i-shi no i-wa-o to*
> *na-ri-te ko-ke no musu made.*

> May thy peaceful reign last long.
> May it last for thousands of years,
> Until this tiny stone will grow
> Into a massive rock, and the moss
> Will cover it deep and thick.

It is a patriotic song that can also be read as a proverb, as a personal credo for endurance. The stone can be the kingdom or it can be a man's life. The moss is the greenery that, in time, will spring even from a rock. In Japan, before the turn of the century, outside my father's house there stood one of those stone lanterns, with four stubby legs and a small pagoda-like roof. Each morning someone in the household would pour a bucketful of water over this lantern, and after several years a skin of living vegetation began to show on the stone. As a boy he was taught that the last line of the anthem refers to a certain type of mossy lichen with exquisitely tiny white flowers sprinkled in amongst the green.

PART TWO

Chapter 12

Manzanar, U.S.A.

In Spanish, Manzanar means "apple orchard." Great stretches of Owens Valley were once green with orchards and alfalfa fields. It has been a desert ever since its water started flowing south into Los Angeles, sometime during the twenties. But a few rows of untended pear and apple trees were still growing there when the camp opened, where a shallow water table had kept them alive. In the spring of 1943 we moved to block 28, right up next to one of the old pear orchards. That's where we stayed until the end of the war, and those trees stand in my memory for the turning of our life in camp, from the outrageous to the tolerable.

Papa pruned and cared for the nearest trees. Late that summer we picked the fruit green and stored it in a root cellar he had dug under our new barracks. At night the wind through the leaves would sound like the surf had sounded in Ocean Park, and while drifting off to sleep I could almost imagine we were still living by the beach.

Mama had set up this move. Block 28 was also

close to the camp hospital. For the most part, people lived there who had to have easy access to it. Mama's connection was her job as dietician. A whole half of one barracks had fallen empty when another family relocated. Mama hustled us in there almost before they'd snapped their suitcases shut.

For all the pain it caused, the loyalty oath finally did speed up the relocation program. One result was a gradual easing of the congestion in the barracks. A shrewd househunter like Mama could set things up fairly comfortably—by Manzanar standards—if she kept her eyes open. But you had to move fast. As soon as the word got around that so-and-so had been cleared to leave, there would be a kind of tribal restlessness, a nervous rise in the level of neighborhood gossip as wives jockeyed for position to see who would get the empty cubicles.

In Block 28 we doubled our living space—four rooms for the twelve of us. Ray and Woody walled them with sheetrock. We had ceilings this time, and linoleum floors of solid maroon. You had three colors to choose from—maroon, black, and forest green— and there was plenty of it around by this time. Some families would vie with one another for the most elegant floor designs, obtaining a roll of each color from the supply shed, cutting it into diamonds, squares, or triangles, shining it with heating oil, then leaving their doors open so that passers-by could admire the handiwork.

Papa brought his still with him when we moved. He set it up behind the door, where he continued to brew his own sake and brandy. He wasn't drinking as much now, though. He spent a lot of time outdoors. Like many of the older Issei men, he didn't take a regular job in camp. He puttered. He had been working hard for thirty years and, bad as it was for him in some ways, camp did allow him time to dabble with hobbies he would never have found time for otherwise.

Once the first year's turmoil cooled down, the authorities started letting us outside the wire for recreation. Papa used to hike along the creeks that channeled down from the base of the Sierras. He brought back chunks of driftwood, and he would pass long hours sitting on the steps carving myrtle limbs into benches, table legs, and lamps, filling our rooms with bits of gnarled, polished furniture.

He hauled stones in off the desert and built a small rock garden outside our doorway, with succulents and a patch of moss. Near it he laid flat steppingstones leading to the stairs.

He also painted watercolors. Until this time I had not known he could paint. He loved to sketch the mountains. If anything made that country habitable it was the mountains themselves, purple when the sun dropped and so sharply etched in the morning light the granite dazzled almost more than the bright snow lacing it. The nearest peaks rose ten thousand feet higher than the valley floor, with Whitney, the highest, just off to the south. They were important for all of us, but especially for the Issei. Whitney reminded Papa of Fujiyama, that is, it gave him the same kind of spiritual sustenance. The tremendous beauty of those peaks was inspirational, as so many natural forms are to the Japanese (the rocks outside our doorway could be those mountains in miniature). They also represented those forces in nature, those powerful and inevitable forces that cannot be resisted, reminding a man that sometimes he must simply endure that which cannot be changed.

Subdued, resigned, Papa's life—all our lives—took on a pattern that would hold for the duration of the war. Public shows of resentment pretty much spent themselves over the loyalty oath crises. *Shikata ga nai* again became the motto, but under altered circumstances. What had to be endured was the climate, the confinement, the steady crumbling away of family life. But the camp itself had been made livable. The government provided for our physical needs. My parents and older brothers and sisters, like most of the internees, accepted their lot and did what they could to make the best of a bad situation. "We're here," Woody would say. "We're here, and there's no use moaning about it forever."

Gardens had sprung up everywhere, in the firebreaks, between the rows of barracks—rock gardens, vegetable gardens, cactus and flower gardens. People who lived in Owens Valley during the war still remember the flowers and lush greenery they could see from the highway as they drove past the main gate. The soil around Manzanar is alluvial and very rich. With water siphoned off from the Los Angeles-bound aqueduct, a large farm was under cultivation just outside the camp, providing the mess halls with lettuce, corn, tomatoes, eggplant, string beans, horseradish, and cucumbers. Near Block 28 some of the men who had been professional gardeners built a small park, with mossy nooks, ponds, waterfalls and curved wooden bridges. Sometimes in the evenings we could walk down the raked gravel paths. You could face away from the barracks, look past a tiny rapids toward the darkening mountains, and for a while not be a prisoner at all. You could hang suspended in some odd, almost lovely land you could not escape from yet almost didn't want to leave.

As the months at Manzanar turned to years, it became a world unto itself, with its own logic and familiar ways. In time, staying there seemed far simpler than moving once again to another, unknown place. It was as if the war were forgotten, our reason for being there forgotten. The present, the little bit of busywork you had right in front of you, became the most urgent thing. In such a narrowed world, in order to survive, you learn to contain your rage and your despair, and you try to re-create, as well as you can, your normality, some sense of things continuing. The fact that America had accused us, or excluded us, or imprisoned us, or whatever it might be called, did not change the kind of world we wanted. Most of us were born in this country; we had no other models. Those parks and gardens lent it an oriental character, but in most ways it was a totally equipped American small town, complete with schools, churches, Boy Scouts, beauty parlors, neighborhood gossip, fire and police departments, glee clubs, softball leagues, Abbott and Costello movies, tennis courts, and traveling shows. (I still remember an Indian who turned up one Saturday billing himself as a Sioux chief, wearing bear claws and head feathers. In the firebreak he sang songs and danced his tribal dances while hundreds of us watched.)

In our family, while Papa puttered, Mama made her daily rounds to the mess halls, helping young mothers with their feeding, planning diets for the various ailments people suffered from. She wore a bright yellow, longbilled sun hat she had made herself and always kept stiffly starched. Afternoons I would see her coming from blocks away, heading home, her tiny figure warped by heat waves and that bonnet a yellow flower wavering in the glare.

In their disagreement over serving the country, Woody and Papa had struck a kind of compromise. Papa talked him out of volunteering; Woody waited for the army to induct him. Meanwhile he clerked in the co-op general store. Kiyo, nearly thirteen by this time, looked forward to the heavy winds. They moved the sand around and uncovered obsidian arrowheads he could sell to old men in camp for fifty cents apiece. Ray, a few years older, played in the six-man touch football league, sometimes against Caucasian teams who would come in from Lone Pine or Independence. My sister Lillian was in high school and singing with a hillbilly band called The Sierra Stars—jeans, cowboy hats, two guitars, and a tub bass. And my oldest brother, Bill, led a dance band called The Jive Bombers—brass and rhythm, with cardboard fold-out music stands lettered J. B. Dances were held every weekend in one of the recreation halls. Bill played trumpet and took vocals on Glenn Miller arrangements of such tunes as *In the Mood, String of Pearls,* and *Don't Fence Me In.* He didn't sing *Don't Fence Me In* out of protest, as if trying quietly to mock the authorities. It just happened to be a hit song one year, and they all wanted to be an up-to-date American swing band. They would blast it out into recreation barracks full of bobbysoxed, jitterbugging couples:

> *Oh, give me land, lots of land*
> *Under starry skies above,*
> *Don't fence me in.*
> *Let me ride through the wide*
> *Open country that I love . . .*

Pictures of the band, in their bow ties and jackets, appeared in the high school yearbook for 1943–1944, along with pictures of just about everything else in camp that year. It was called *Our World.* In its pages you see school kids with armloads of books, wearing cardigan sweaters and walking past rows of tarpapered shacks. You see chubby girl yell leaders, pompons flying as they leap with glee. You read about the school play, called *Growing Pains* ". . . the story of a typical American home, in this case that of the McIntyres. They see their boy and girl tossed into the normal awkward growing up stage, but can offer little assistance or direction in their turbulent course . . ." with Shoji Katayama as George McIntyre, Takudo Ando as Terry McIntyre, and Mrs. McIntyre played by Kazuko Nagai.

All the class pictures are in there, from the seventh grade through twelfth, with individual head shots of seniors, their names followed by the names of the high schools they would have graduated from on the outside: Theodore Roosevelt, Thomas Jefferson, Herbert Hoover, Sacred Heart. You see pretty girls on bicycles, chicken yards full of fat pullets, patients back-tilted in dental chairs, lines of laundry, and finally, two large blowups, the first of a high tower with a searchlight, against a Sierra backdrop, the next a two-age endsheet showing a wide path that curves among rows of elm trees. White stones border the path. Two dogs are following an old woman in gardening clothes as she strolls along. She is in the middle distance, small beneath the trees, beneath the snowy peaks. It is winter. All the elms are bare. The scene is both stark and comforting. This path leads toward one edge of camp, but the wire is out of sight, or out of focus. The tiny woman seems very much at ease. She and her tiny dogs seem almost swallowed by the landscape, or floating in it.

Chapter 13

Outings, Explorations

Once we settled into Block 28 that ache I'd felt since soon after we arrived at Manzanar subsided. It didn't entirely disappear, but it gradually submerged, as semblances of order returned and our pattern of life assumed its new design.

For one thing, Kiyo and I and all the other children finally had *a school*. During the first year, teachers had been volunteers; equipment had been makeshift; classes were scattered all over camp, in mess halls, recreation rooms, wherever we could be squeezed in. Now a teaching staff had been hired. Two blocks were turned into Manzanar High, and a third block of fifteen barracks was set up to house the elementary grades. We had blackboards, new desks, reference books, lab supplies. That second, stable school year was one of the things *Our World* commemorated when it came out in June of 1944.

My days spent in classrooms are largely a blur now, as one merges into another. What I see clearly is the face of my fourth-grade teacher—a pleasant face, but completely invulnerable, it seemed to me at the time, with sharp, commanding eyes. She came from Kentucky. She wore wedgies, loose slacks, and sweaters that were too short in the sleeves. A tall, heavyset spinster, about forty years old, she always wore a scarf on her head, tied beneath the chin, even during class, and she spoke with a slow, careful Appalachian accent. She was probably the best teacher I've ever had—strict, fairminded, dedicated to her job. Because of her, when we finally returned to the outside world I was, academically at least, more than prepared to keep up with my peers.

I see her face. But what I hear, still ringing in my mind's ear, is the Glee Club I belonged to, made up of girls from the fourth, fifth, and sixth grades. We rehearsed every day during the last period. In concert we wore white cotton blouses and dark skirts. Forty voices strong we would line up at assemblies or at talent shows in the firebreak and sing out in unison all the favorites school kids used to learn: *Beautiful Dreamer, Down By the Old Mill Stream, Shine On Harvest Moon, Battle Hymn of the Republic*.

Outside of school we had a recreation program, with leaders hired by the War Relocation Authority. During the week they organized games and craft activities. On weekends we often took hikes beyond the fence. A series of picnic groups and camping sites had been built by internees—clearings, with tables, benches, and toilets. The first was about half a mile out, the farthest several miles into the Sierras. As restrictions gradually loosened, you could measure your liberty by how far they'd let you go—to Camp Three with a Caucasian, to Camp Three alone, to Camp Four with a Caucasian, to Camp Four alone. As fourth- and fifth-graders we usually hiked out to Camp One, on the edge of Bair's Creek, where we could wade, collect rocks, and sit on the bank eating lunches the mess hall crew packed for us. I would always take along a quart jar and a white handkerchief and sit for an hour next to the stream, watching it strain through the cloth, trickling under the glass. Water there was the clearest I've ever seen, running right down off the snow.

One of our leaders on those excursions was a pretty young woman named Lois, about twenty-five at the time, who wore long braids, full skirts, and peasant blouses. She was a Quaker, like so many of the Caucasians who came in to teach and do volunteer work. She also had a crush on a tall, very handsome and popular Nisei boy who sometimes sang and danced in the talent shows. His name was Isao. In order to find a little free time together, Lois and Isao arranged an overnight camping trip for all the girls in our class. We took jars for water, potatoes to roast, and army blankets and hiked up Bair's Creek one Friday afternoon to a nice little knoll at the base of the mountains.

All the girls were tittering and giggling at the way Isao and Lois held hands and looked at each other. They built us a big driftwood fire that night, and told us ghost stories until they figured we had all dozed off. Then they disappeared for a while into the sagebrush. I was still awake and heard their careful footsteps snapping twigs. I thought how hard it would be to walk around out there without a flashlight. It was years later that I remembered and understood what that outing must have been for them. At the time I had my own escape to keep me occupied. In truth, I barely noticed their departure. This was the first overnight camping trip I'd ever made. For me it was enough to be outside the barracks for a night, outside the square mile of wire, next to a crackling blaze and looking at stars so thick and so close to the ground I could have reached up and scooped out an armful.

If I had been told, the next morning, that I could stay outside the fence as long as I wanted, that I was free to go, it would have sent me sprinting for the compound. Lovely as they were to look at, the Sierras were frightening to think about, an icy barricade. If you took off in the opposite direction and made it past the Inyos, you'd hit Death Valley, while to the south there loomed a range of brown, sculpted hills everyone said were full of rattlesnakes. Camp One was about as far as I cared to venture. What's more, Block 28 was "where I lived" now. One night was plenty, one night every once in a while, to explore whatever was out there.

You might call that the image for a whole series of little explorations I began to make during the next year, looking for some place "outside," early gropings for that special thing I could be or do for myself.

In addition to the regular school sessions and the recreation program, classes of every kind were being offered all over camp: singing, acting, trumpet playing, tap-dancing, plus traditional Japanese arts like needlework, judo, and kendo. The first class I attended was in baton twirling, taught by a chubby girl about fourteen named Nancy. In the beginning I used a sawed-off broomstick with an old tennis ball stuck on one end. When it looked like I was going to keep at this, Mama ordered me one like Nancy's from the Sears, Roebuck catalogue. Nancy was a very good twirler and taught us younger kids all her tricks. For months I practiced, joined the baton club at school, and even entered contests. Since then I have often wondered what drew me to it at that age. I wonder, because of all the activities I tried out in camp, this was the one I stayed with, in fact returned to almost obsessively when I entered high school in southern California a few years later. By that time I was desperate to be "accepted," and baton twirling was one trick I could perform that was thoroughly, unmistakably American—putting on the boots and a dress crisscrossed with braid, spinning the silver stick and tossing it high to the tune of a John Philip Sousa march.

Even at ten, before I really knew what waited outside, the Japanese in me could not compete with that. It tried—in camp, and many times later, in one form or another. My visit to the old geisha who lived across the firebreak was a typical example of how those attempts turned out. She was offering lessons in the traditional dancing called *odori*. A lot of young girls studied this in order to take part in the big *obon* festival held every August, a festival honoring dead ancestors, asking them to bring good crops in the fall.

She was about seventy, a tiny, aristocratic-looking woman. She took students in her barracks cubicle, which was fitted out like a little Buddhist shrine, with tatami mats on the floor. She would kneel in her kimono and speak very softly in Japanese, while her young assistant would gracefully swing closed knees or bend her swanlike neck to the old geisha's instructions.

I sat across the room from her for an hour trying to follow what was going on. It was all a mystery. I had never learned the language. And this woman was so old, even her dialect was foreign to me. She seemed an occult figure, more spirit than human. When she bowed to me from her knees at the end of the hour, I rushed out of there, back to more familiar sur-roundings.

Something about her fascinated me though. For a while I tried to keep in contact with her lore via the reports of two girls from my class, Reiko and Mitsue, who had stayed on as students. Because they came from wealthy families and spoke and understood both English and Japanese, they had high opinions of themselves. Whenever I pressed them for details of what they'd learned, they would tease me.

"A good dancer must have good skin," Reiko would say. "In order to have good skin you must rub Rose Brilliantine Hair Tonic on your face and rub cold cream in your hair."

I went home and did this secretly, when no one else was around, and waited for my skin to become the skin of an odori dancer.

"You have to think about your clothing," Mitsue would tell me. "A good dancer is recognized by her clothing. You should wear your stockings inside out and never, *never* wear any underpants."

I did this too, on the sly, until Mama asked me why my socks were always inside out, and why I was wearing nothing underneath my dress. She was not amused when I explained it to her. She told me to stay away from those girls, they were just being mean, and if I wanted lessons from the old geisha woman, Mama herself would take me over there and arrange it. I shook my head and told her no, I didn't want to do that right now. I had another kind of dancing in mind.

This time it was ballet. I had never seen ballet. I'd only heard of it. But it sounded like something I would want to do. In Ocean Park I had taken tap-dancing lessons; my older brothers would coax me to perform for visitors, and it gained me a lot of attention. In camp I had already danced in a couple of talent shows. When the word came around that a woman was offering ballet lessons, I showed up, with three other young girls. It was a dusty day anyhow, and there wasn't much you could do outside.

The classroom was an abandoned barracks. No one had lived there for months. Light showed through the warped planking. It was almost like going back two years to the day we first arrived, except that a piano sat on the bare, splintered boards, and here was a thirtyish Japanese woman, with her hair pulled back in a chignon, wearing a pink tutu, a pair of pink toe-dancing shoes, and no tights.

At the piano sat a young girl with glasses on, studying some sheet music in the not quite adequate light from a single overhead bulb. When we were all in the room and seated on the floor, she began to play, and the dancer began to dance as if she were the one trying out, not us. She twirled, and she leaped from wall to wall, flinging her arms. She had been a good dancer once, but now she was overweight, and sad to watch, even in the eyes of a ten-year-old who had never seen this kind of dancing.

I was intrigued by her strange, flat-toed shoes, badly frayed, worn down by the boards. I stared too at her legs. I could not stop watching them while she spun, sidestepping knotholes. They were thick, white, blueveined, tapering sharply from the quivering thighs, the kind of legs my older sisters would have called *daikon ashi* (*daikon* means horseradish; *ashi* is leg).

She began to show us a few steps and tricks, beginning with the splits. She hoisted herself and reversed her torso and came down again with her legs spread. I winced, sure the planks would tear her skin. Then she got the four of us up to try first position, which I did mainly out of courtesy, in order not to hurt the feelings of this heavy woman with her *daikon ashi* and her shredded shoes.

After showing us the first three ballet positions she sat down to rest. She took her shoes off. Her toes were showing blood. I noticed then the lines in her face, the traces of gray in her black hair. I felt so sorry for her I decided to go ahead and sign up for her course. But once I left that room, back out into the dusty, windflurried afternoon, I never did return. Ballet seemed then some terrible misuse of the body, and she was so anxious to please us, her very need to hold on to whatever she had been scared me away.

Among my explorations during these months, there was one more, final venture into Catholicism. The Maryknoll chapel was just up the street now and easy to get to. I resumed my catechism. Once again I was listening with rapt terror to the lives of the saints and the martyrs, although that wasn't really what attracted me this time. I had found another kind of inspiration, had seen another way the church might make me into something quite extraordinary.

I had watched a girl my own age shining at the center of one of their elaborate ceremonies. It appealed to me tremendously. She happened to be an orphan, and I figured that if this much could befall an orphan, imagine how impressive *I* would look in such a role.

I had long observed her from a distance, a slim and lovely girl, and always aloof, because of the way other kids treated orphans there, as if a lack of parents put you somehow beneath everyone else. I confess I felt that way myself. Orphans were in a class apart. In Block 28 we saw them often. "Children's Village," where Sister Suzanne and Sister Bernadette put in a good deal of time, was as near to us as their chapel— two blocks away in the opposite direction. Each day about a dozen of them, including this girl, would come trooping past our barracks on the way to a catechism lesson. On days I intended to go, I would wait till they were half a block ahead, so I wouldn't be seen arriving in their midst.

This girl had already been baptized. What I witnessed was her confirmation. She was dressed like a bride, in a white gown, white lace hood, and sheer veil, walking toward the altar, down the aisle of that converted barracks. Watching her from the pew I was pierced with envy for the position she had gained. At the same time I was filled with awe and with a startled wonder at the notion that this girl, this orphan, could become such a queen.

A few days later I let it be known that I was going to be baptized into the church and confirmed as soon as the nuns thought I was ready. I announced this to the Sisters and they rejoiced. I announced it at home, and Papa exploded.

"No," he roared. "Absolutely not!"

I just stood there, stunned, too scared to speak.

"You're too young!"

I started to cry.

"How are you going to get married?" he shouted. "If you get baptized a Catholic, you have to marry a Catholic. No Japanese boys are in the Catholic church. You get baptized now, how are you going to find a good Japanese boy to marry?"

I ran to Mama, but she knew better than to argue with him about this. I ran to the chapel and told Sister Bernadette, and she came hurrying to the barracks. She and Papa had become pretty good friends over the months. Once every week or so she would visit, and while he sipped his apricot brandy they would talk about religion. But this time, when she came to the door and called *"Wakatsuki-san?"* he met her there shouting, "No! No baptism!"

She raised her eyebrows, trying to stare him down.

He rose to his full height, as if she, about the size of Mama, were the general of some invading army, and said, "Too young!"

"Old enough to know God!"

"Who knows anything of God at ten?"

This made her angry. At any other time they would have taken an hour hearing each other out. But now, when she opened her mouth to reply, his upheld flat palm stopped her. He was not going to argue. He wouldn't even let her past the door.

In exasperation she glared at him, then turned and walked away. I ran to my bunk, devastated, and wept, hating him. I was too ashamed to go back to catechism after that. I just hated Papa, for weeks, and dreamed of the white-gowned princess I might have become. Late afternoons, practicing my baton in the firebreak, angrily I would throw him into the air and watch him twirl, and catch him, and throw him high, again and again and again.

Chapter 14

In the Firebreak

He was right, of course. I did not know what I was getting myself into. Years later I silently thanked him for forcing me to postpone such decisions until I was old enough to think for myself. But at the time it was unforgivable. And it was typical of his behavior during those days. He had no boat crew to command, no income to manage, no trips to plan, not even a dining table to preside over. He would putter blandly along, then suddenly, unexpectedly, as if to remind himself he was still in charge of something, he would burst out like that, his intentions right, but his manner stubborn and relentless, forcing distances between us.

As his youngest child I had grown up blessed with special attentions. Now, more and more I found myself cut off from him. When I needed reassurance I would get it from Woody or Chizu, or from Mama, who had more of herself to give by this time. Then one afternoon there came a moment when I was cut off from both of them, Papa and Mama together. It wasn't loneliness I felt, or isolation; they were still within reach. Rather, it was that first, brief flicker of total separateness. It could have occurred anywhere we might have been living; I had reached the age. This scene happened to be set in one of the firebreaks at Manzanar.

My oldest sister Eleanor figures in it. She lay in the camp hospital, trying to give birth to a baby she had thought she'd be having in Reno, Nevada, where she and her husband Shig had relocated in 1943. Through friends they had found a house there, and Shig lined up a job in a restaurant. Early in 1944 the government decided that Nisei should be eligible for Selective Service, like all other American citizens. A few months later Shig was drafted. Eleanor, pregnant, could find neither work nor money enough to pay for having a baby. She couldn't stay in Reno and she couldn't go with Shig to the army's training camp in Louisiana, so she voluntarily re-entered camp.

When she went into the hospital, it was a time of great anxiety in our family. Two of my other sisters had borne children there. They had both hemorrhaged badly, and blood plasma was in short supply, our needs being low on the wartime priority list. One sister might have died had not Woody provided blood by direct transfusion. In the case of a sister-in-law of ours, who had miscarried and hemorrhaged, no one was able to arrest it in time, and she just bled to death in her hospital bed.

These memories were very much with us. Papa, in particular, was worried. Eleanor was his oldest daughter, and this was her first child. Her husband had gone to Germany with an infantry division, and now she was struggling through the second day of a difficult labor. He and Mama were taking turns sitting with her. And what I remember, late the second afternoon, is Mama running toward us from the other side of the firebreak. I was walking with Papa, as he started out for the hospital, and here she came, small, and running, all bundled up—it was December— shouting, "Ko! Ko!" making little puffs of frost in the icy air.

I looked at Papa, and his face had filled with terror. He tried to run to meet her, but couldn't, could barely keep his stride. His look filled me with terror too. I was sure Eleanor had died in the hospital. Our fear must have held back Mama's progress. It seemed we watched her run for minutes across that stretch of cleared sand. There was room enough for a football game, or an entire parade. In my eyes then, it was a threatening openness, a no man's land.

We met her in the sand, Mama breathless, small in front of him, looking up saying, "Ko! Ko, it's a boy!"

His face gave way. His eyes filled. "A boy!"

"Yes!"

"And Eleanor?"

"Yes. Okay!"

"Okay."

"They're both okay."

His tears let go, unchecked. Mama was already crying. She began to talk excitedly, jabbering the details. As the news sunk in, my fear was replaced by an odd detachment. The burden fell away, leaving me afloat, and I was a spectator witnessing the nearest to a love scene I would ever see between them. My own perception removed me from it. I was more awed than aware, but I knew whatever I was watching was somehow both tender and profound, with an intimacy that made me invisible to them.

Papa put an arm around her, needing her support. He was wearing the rust-colored turtleneck sweater he used to take on fishing trips, the one she had knitted for him before the war. Now, as she talked, the fingers of one hand played over its yarn, as if inspecting her own workmanship. While the late sun turned this rusty sweater dark shades of orange, they stood there in the great expanse of the firebreak, far out from the rows of barracks, weeping with relief and happiness, talking quietly, just the two of them.

Chapter 15

Departures

In the months to come they would draw together even more closely, just as I would hold to them—my moment of separateness a foreshadowing, but not yet a reality. Our family had begun to dwindle, along with the entire camp population. By the end of 1944 about 6,000 people remained, and those, for the most part, were the aging and the young. Whoever had prospects on the outside, and the energy to go, was leaving, relocating, or entering military service. No one could blame them. To most of the Nisei, anything looked better than remaining in camp. For many of their parents, just the opposite was true.

Eleanor and Shig had been the first of my family to leave. A few months after she had her baby, she moved back to Reno to stay with friends there. The next to go was Woody who, in August 1944, had been drafted. When the notice came he showed it to Papa.

"And now what will you do?" Papa said glumly.

"I have to go."

"What if you refused to answer the letter?"

"It's my duty."

"What about those twenty-six boys from Tule Lake who refused to report? The judge in San Francisco ruled that they were right. It was in the papers. You can't lock somebody up because he might be disloyal, and then make him join the army. That was the judge's conclusion."

"Well, right now Tom Dobashi who used to live over in Block Nine is in jail in Los Angeles for refusing to report for his physical."

"He was already in jail."

Woody blinked, missing the point at first. Then he grinned. "C'mon, Pop. It's not that bad out here. Not anymore."

"Then why don't you stay?"

"I'm gonna stay. For a while. Until they call me up. They put me in the reserve unit in camp. It could be months. Maybe the war will be over by then."

His unit was called up in November. We all went down to see them off at the main gate—nineteen young men in their teens and twenties, some wearing suits and ties, some, like Woody, wearing overcoats and neck scarves against the cold, carrying satchels, traveling bags, shaving kits. They lined up two deep for a photo that ran later in the camp paper. Then we watched Woody join the shuffling line and climb aboard.

For me it was almost like watching Papa leave again. I didn't know where he was going or understand quite why. When his bus pulled out I only knew that if anything happened to him the world would probably be coming to an end, because *nothing* could happen to Woody. He had always been so solid. I hugged Mama while we watched his final wave through the window, his mustache lifting above that impish smile, as if we had all just pulled a fast one on the world.

Chizu was with us, waving back. This made it almost like the day, three years earlier, we had watched the boats sail out of San Pedro Harbor, except that Chizu had two children now, and instead of a handful of fishermen's wives, there were 500 others with us here. They had turned out, like people in small towns all over the country, to watch their young men leave. The 442nd Combat Regiment was famous now, full of heroes, fighting in Europe to help the Allies win the war, and showing that Niseis too could be patriots. Woody was that kind of Nisei, anxious to prove to the world his loyalty, his manhood, something about his family honor. Climbing aboard he must have been thinking of those things, while Mama, no doubt, was thinking of the mother at Manzanar who had already received a posthumous Congressional Medal of Honor on behalf of her son who'd been killed in Italy.

In these ways it was a typical wartime departure, full of proud smiles and half-concealed worry. In other ways it was edged with unique uncertainties. Families were being further torn asunder, and those left behind knew no more about their own fate than they did of the loved ones moving on. Would we still be here after the war? Would we be living forever in the summer heat and winter wind of Owens Valley? And if not here, then where else?

The answers to these questions, when they came, only added to our insecurity.

Chapter 16

Free to Go

The answers began with a Supreme Court ruling that December, in the case called *Ex Parte Endo*. It was the last of three key cases heard since the camps had opened.

In the first, Gordon Hirabayashi, a Nisei student from the University of Washington, challenged the evacuation order. He had also violated the army's curfew, imposed early in 1942 on all west-coast Japanese. He challenged the racial bias of these actions and the abuse of his civil rights. The court avoided the issue of the evacuation itself by ruling on the curfew. It upheld the army's decision to limit the movements of a racially select group of citizens. The reasoning: wartime necessity.

In the second case, the issue was the exclusion orders that removed us from our homes and sent us inland. Fred Korematsu, a young Nisei living in Oakland, had ignored the evacuation to stay with his Caucasian girlfriend. He had plastic surgery done on his face, he changed his name, and was posing as a Spanish Hawaiian when the FBI caught up with him.

In court, the racial bias was challenged again. Why were no German Americans evacuated, it was asked, or Americans of Italian descent? Weren't these nations our enemies too? Due process had been violated, Korematsu claimed, along with other constitutional rights. But the army's decision to evacuate was also upheld by the Supreme Court.

The final case challenged the internment itself. Soon after she was evacuated, in April 1942, Mitsue Endo, a twenty-one-year-old Nisei and an employee of the California State Highway Commission, had filed a petition for habeas corpus, protesting her detention at Topaz Camp in central Utah. She spent two and a half years awaiting the high court's decision, which was that she had been right: the government cannot detain loyal citizens against their will.

Anticipating this ruling, the army's Western Defense Command had already announced that the mass exclusion orders of 1942 were being rescinded. Next it was announced that all the camps would be closed within the coming twelve months and that internees now had the right to return to their former homes.

In our family the response to this news was hardly joyful. For one thing we had no home to return to. Worse, the very thought of going back to the west coast filled us with dread. What will they think of us, those who sent us here? How will they look at us? Three years of wartime propaganda—racist headlines, atrocity movies, hate slogans, and fright-mask posters—had turned the Japanese face into something despicable and grotesque. Mama and Papa knew this. They had been reading the papers. Even I knew this, although it was not until many years later that I realized how bad things actually were.

In addition to the traditionally racist organizations like the American Legion and The Native Sons of The Golden West, who had been agitating against the westcoast Japanese for decades, new groups had sprung up during the war, with the specific purpose of preventing anyone of Japanese descent from returning to the coast—groups like No Japs Incorporated in San Diego, The Home Front Commandoes in Sacramento, and the Pacific Coast Japanese Problem League in Los Angeles. Also, some growers' associations, threatened by the return of interned farmers, had been using the war as a way to foment hostile feelings in the major farming areas.

What's more, our years of isolation at Manzanar had widened the already spacious gap between the races, and it is not hard to understand why so many preferred to stay where they were. Before the war one of the standard charges made against the Japanese was their clannishness, their standoffishness, their refusal to assimilate. The camps had made this a reality in the extreme. After three years in our desert ghetto, at least we knew where we stood with our neighbors, could live more or less at ease with them.

Yet now the government was saying we not only were free to go; like the move out of Terminal Island, and the move to Owens Valley, we had to go. Definite dates were being fixed for the closing of the camp.

By January of '45 a few determined internees were already trying to recover former homes and farmlands. Ominous reports of their reception began trickling back, to confirm our deepest fears. A Nisei man had been assaulted on the street in Seattle. A home was burned in San Jose. Nightriders carrying shotguns had opened fire on a farmhouse near Fresno, narrowly missing two sleeping children. Later on, in May, one of my sisters and her husband, leaving for the east, were escorted to the Southern Pacific depot in Los Angeles by armed guards, not because they were thought to be dangerous, but for their own protection.

Most of the Japanese returning to the coast resettled without suffering bodily harm. But gossip tends to thrive on bad news, not good. Stories such as these spread through the camp and grew in our minds like tumors. I remember hearing them discussed in our barracks, quietly, as if Ku Klux Klansmen lurked outside the window, the same way my brothers discussed our dilemma during the brief stay in Boyle Heights, before the evacuation.

I would listen to the stories and I would cringe. And this was both odd and confusing to me, because ever since we'd arrived, the outside world had loomed in my imagination as someplace inaccessible yet wonderfully desirable. I would recall our days in Ocean Park. I would flip through the Sears, Roebuck catalogue, dreaming of the dresses and boots and coats that were out there somewhere at the other end of the highway beyond the gate. All the truly good things, it often seemed, the things we couldn't get, were outside, and had to be sent for, or shipped in. In this sense, God and the Sears, Roebuck catalogue were pretty much one and the same in my young mind.

Once, during a novena at the Maryknoll chapel, I had asked for something I desperately longed for and had never seen inside the camp. We were told to ask for something we really wanted. We were to write it on a piece of paper, pray devoutly for nine days, and if we'd prayed well it would be answered. The nuns expected us to ask for purity of soul, or a holy life. I asked God for some dried apricots. I wrote this on a piece of paper, dropped it into the prayer box, and began to fantasize about how they would arrive, in a package from Sears, Roebuck. I knew how they would taste, and feel in my hands. I said my rosary, thirty times a day, for nine days, and for nine more days after that I waited. The dried apricots never came. My faith in God and in the Catholic church slipped several notches at that time. But not my faith in *the outside,* where all such good things could be found. I went back to flipping through the catalogue.

Those images, of course, had come from my past. What I had to face now, a year later, was the future. I was old enough to imagine it, and also old enough to fear it. The physical violence didn't trouble me. Somehow I didn't quite believe that, or didn't want to believe such things could happen to *us.* It was the humiliation. That continuous, unnamed ache I had been living with was precise and definable now. Call it the foretaste of being hated. I knew ahead of time that if someone looked at me with hate, I would have to allow it, to swallow it, because something in me, something about me deserved it. At ten I saw that coming, like a judge's sentence, and I would have stayed inside the camp forever rather than step outside and face such a moment.

I shared this particular paralysis with Mama and Papa, but not with my older brothers and sisters. The hostility worried them. But their desire to be rid of Manzanar outweighed that worry. They were in their twenties and had their lives to lead. They decided to take a chance on the east coast. It was 3,000 miles away, with no history of anti-Orientalism, in fact no Oriental history at all. So few people of Asian ancestry had settled there, it was like heading for a neutral country.

Bill was the first to make that move, with Tomi and their baby boy. He had lined up a job with Seabrook

Farms in New Jersey, a new frozen-food enterprise that offered work to many Nisei at the end of the war. A few weeks later Frances and her husband joined them, followed by Martha and Kaz, then Lillian, who was just finishing her junior year in high school, and Ray.

As each cluster of relatives departed we'd say, "See you in New Jersey. Find us all a big house back there."

What we told each other was that Bill and Frances and the others would go on ahead, make sure things could be worked out, then they'd send for the rest of us. "See you in New Jersey," we would wave, as the bus pulled out taking someone else to the train station in L.A. But they all knew, even as they said it, that Papa would never move back east. As bad as the west coast sounded, it was still his home territory. He was too old to start over, too afraid of rejection in an unknown part of the world, too stubborn and too tired to travel that far, and finally too proud to do piecework on an assembly line. Like so many Issei, he had, for better or worse, run his own businesses, been his own man for too long to tolerate the idea of working for someone else.

The truth was, at this point Papa did not know which way to turn. In the government's eyes a free man now, he sat, like those black slaves you hear about who, when they got word of their freedom at the end of the Civil War, just did not know where else to go or what else to do and ended up back on the plantation, rooted there out of habit or lethargy or fear.

Chapter 17

It's All Starting Over

In June the schools were closed for good. After a final commencement exercise the teachers were dismissed. The high school produced a second yearbook, *Valediction 1945,* summing up its years in camp. The introduction shows a page-wide photo of a forearm and hand squeezing pliers around a length of taut barbed wire strung beneath one of the towers. Across the page runs the caption, "From Our World . . . through these portals . . . to new horizons."

That summer the farm outside the fence gradually shut down. Cultivation stopped. Crops in the ground were harvested as they ripened. Nothing new was planted. They began to auction off the tractors, the trucks and tools.

Then the word went out that the entire camp would close without fail by December 1. Those who did not choose to leave voluntarily would be scheduled for resettlement in weekly quotas. Once you were scheduled, you could choose a place—a state, a city, a town—and the government would pay your way there. If you didn't choose, they'd send you back to the community you lived in before you were evacuated.

Papa gave himself up to the schedule. The government had put him here, he reasoned, the government could arrange his departure. What could he lose by waiting? Outside he had no job to go back to. A California law passed in 1943 made it illegal now for Issei to hold commercial fishing licenses. And his boats and nets were gone, he knew—confiscated or stolen. Here in camp he had shelter. The women and children still with him had enough to eat. He decided to sit it out as long as he could.

That August, as usual, it was brutally hot. He would sit in the shade on our barracks steps in his undershirt, reading the papers, reading aloud sometimes, to Mama and Granny, as he had done for his fellow inmates at Fort Lincoln, filling them in on the state of the world. He would read about Japan's losses during those final weeks of the Pacific war and claim he had predicted it. He would read about the Russians moving into Korea and grumble that if the Americans occupied Japan there'd be another war within ten years, maybe five. He would read about the housing shortage all along the west coast, brought on by wartime population growth, and he would throw the paper down in disgust.

"Aaagghh!"

"Why do you read the papers?" Mama would say. "It always makes you go aaagghh."

"They have been so busy building tanks and bombers, they have run out of houses for everyone to live in."

"It's the war," Mama said.

"So where do they think they are going to put people like us?"

"I was in the washroom this morning, and Akiko

told me it is just like nineteen forty-two all over again. She got a letter from her sister in Los Angeles. Japanese people coming back from the camps are being put into trailers and Quonset huts. We should have left here when there were still houses to live in."

"You are the one who wanted to wait," Papa snapped.

"I said for a while."

"For a while." He mimicked her.

"So did you."

He raised his voice. "You said it would be too hard on the kids."

"You said so yourself."

He shouted, rearing back to challenge her. "Then don't tell me we waited too long!"

Mama's eyes closed, squinting tight, shutting off the conversation. Her face became a web of creases.

"Jeannie," she said to me. "Come over here. *Momo* my back a little bit."

I was out there with them, in the shade in my shorts and barefooted, waiting for what little coolness might come at us through the pear trees. Most of the recreation leaders were gone by this time. Since the school closed, I had been running loose, and yet not running very far at all, sticking closer to our barracks now than ever before. I stood up and started massaging her shoulders.

"Harder," she said. "There's a knot someplace. I can feel it all the way up my neck, all around behind my eyes."

I started pounding with my fists, like little pistons. Sometimes Kiyo and I would take turns doing this, up and down her back. Today, even the fists wouldn't satisfy.

Gruffly Papa said, "Hey! You move over, Jeannie! Get outta the way." He swung a leg behind Mama and sat down on the step above, digging his thumbs into the thick flesh below her neck.

Breath hissed in through her teeth. She let out two tiny groans. "Unh. Unh."

He asked her, "What did Doctor Matsui say?"

"I didn't see him."

"Where was he?"

"He was there, but it was too crowded. I'm going back later. The whole hallway was filled up. Everybody has a headache, or a stomach ache, or a backache that cannot be explained. Everybody is sick. Everything is like nineteen forty-two. It is all starting over."

"Hey!" he ordered. "You want a back rub? Sit up straight!"

He ground his elbow into the base of her neck, pushing it down her spine. Her groans got louder.

"Ooh. Ooh. That's it. That's almost it."

"Listen," he said. "Maybe we will not have to leave so soon. Last night at the block leaders meeting it was definitely decided that the camp *must* remain open until everyone has a place to go back to."

"What does the administration say?"

"The block leaders are preparing a statement to take to them."

"Do you think it will do any good?"

Papa did not answer. He was dragging his elbow slowly up one spinal muscle and staring down the street, where the answer to her question was everywhere pathetically evident. Leaves and windfall pears had piled up beneath the trees. In the park nearby, grass creepers edged out into the graveled paths. Little clusters of debris were slowing down the waterways. All around, you saw these signals of neglect, as if the camp itself were slowly, deliberately disintegrating in order to comply with the administration's deadline. Every day another barracks or two would fall empty. The outer blocks had long been deserted, filling up with tumbleweeds and sand. Right next to our stairs, in Papa's rock garden, the moss was dry, the sand needed raking. No one bothered with it.

Mama said, "Ko."

No answer.

"Ko?"

"What?"

"What are we going to do?"

"Wait."

"For what?" she asked.

"Listen to me. I have an idea. All these people who are waiting in the hall to see Doctor Matsui, they are worried about where they are going to live and how they are going to make money on the outside. Is that not so?"

"Yes."

"Suppose we organize some kind of a cooperative. For Japanese people coming back from the camps. We will design a housing project, and all the men looking for work will build houses."

"You have to have some land for that," Mama said.

"Of course."

"You have to have money."

"We will get a loan from the government. At the block leaders meeting it was decided that they *must* provide low-interest loans for families returning from the camps. They cannot deprive us of our homes and our fishing boats and our automobiles and lock us up for three years and then just turn us loose into the cities again. They have to help us get a new start."

"Is this too in the statement they are preparing?"

"Yes. They deliver it at noon today."

"Do you think the government will do anything?"

Again, Papa did not answer. They both knew what it would be. This time his long pause slipped into pure silence. Without the answer he could continue dabbling with the dream. Mama's eyes squinted shut. His fingers worked below her shoulder blades. He had found the knot, the tension node, and he homed in on it with a practiced knuckle. Mama rolled her head from side to side, pulling at the tendons in her neck, groaning loudly now, hissing with the painful pleasure of his cure.

The last hope that something might postpone our returning to the outside world was extinguished on August 6 when the atomic bomb fell on Hiroshima. That ended the Second World War. America had won. Internment camps were undeniably a thing of the past.

I remember seeing the newspaper photos of the mushroom cloud that bloomed above the city and hearing the murmurs that rose ever so quietly from the stunned, almost reverent hush all over camp. The unbelievable horror of what had happened was not yet known. This was as strange, as awesome, as mysteriously unnerving as Pearl Harbor had been. And in the same way that the first attack finished off one period in our lives, so this appalling climax marked the end of another.

Nine days later, all over America people were dancing in the streets. At Manzanar I suppose there was some rejoicing too. At least we were no longer *the enemy*. But the atomic bombing, if anything, just sharpened our worry. I still see Papa sitting on our steps for long hours, smoking cigarettes in his ivory holder, staring into the mountains he went to with his eyes whenever he needed sustenance. Here he sat, a man without prospects, perhaps now without even a family in Japan to confirm his own history, fifty-eight years old, and his children scattered across the land: Woody in the army at Fort Douglas, Utah; Eleanor in Reno; her husband in Germany with the occupation troops; Bill and Martha and Frances and Lillian in New Jersey; Ray now in the Coast Guard, the only service that would take him at the age of seventeen.

Papa read the papers and studied the changeless peaks, while all around us other families were moving out, forcing our name ever higher on the list. Every day busloads left from the main gate, heading south with their quotas, filled with Mamas and Papas and Grannies who had postponed movement as long as possible, and soldiers' wives like Chizu, and children like Kiyo and May and me, too young yet to be out on our own. Some of the older folks resisted leaving right up to the end and had to have their bags packed for them and be physically lifted and shoved onto the buses. When our day finally arrived, in early October, there were maybe 2,000 people still living out there, waiting their turn and hoping it wouldn't come.

Chapter 18

Ka-ke, Near Hiroshima: April 1946

On a low hill the gravestones tilt crazily, as if trying to wrench loose from the soil.

"It was the bomb," Toyo explains. "Even here, fifteen miles away, like an earthquake sent to rip the world in two."

Woody, gazing at the stones, says, "Were many in our family lost?"

"We were lucky," Toyo says. "Only one. He would have been your cousin. None of the rest of us were in the city then."

"And is he buried here?"

"No. He was near the center of the fire storm. But let us not talk of that. I did not bring you here to talk of that. Do you see this stone?"

"This one?"

"Your father was buried here in nineteen thirteen."

Woody looks at her, wondering how old she really is, wondering how well she remembers. She is Papa's aunt. She must be eighty. He studies her face for some measure of how far her recollection can be trusted. He *thinks of Granny, not yet this old, but blind, forgetful, full of needs that must be cared for and tales everyone half listens to. Toyo's not at all like that. She has a monk's tranquillity. Her eyes are still alert. Her face shows both the burden and the full understanding of all her eighty years or more.*

With great care Woody says, "But I told you, he lives in California now, today, alive, with ten children, of which I am the second oldest."

"In nineteen thirteen he had been gone for nine years, with no word. To the family in Japan, he was dead. This is his gravestone. I show it to you so you will know how much he mattered to us here, so you will know how happy you have made me bringing this news that he still lives. The happiness I feel now erases all this war has put us through."

Woody looks away, tears welling in his eyes. He stares at the stone, the characters engraved on it. When he looks back at Toyo he expects to see her weeping. She isn't. She gazes intently at him, as if he is ready to disappear, as if to imprint him in her mind before he's gone.

"Come," she says. "We don't want to linger here. There are many things to see, many relatives to meet. Everyone will want to see Ko's son."

Woody has postponed this visit many times, postponed the train ride south from Tokyo, afraid of how he'd be received. Being an American is hard enough; being a Nisei among these occupying forces is sometimes agony. He dreads those looks that seem to call him traitor to his homeland or his race. And if he sees such looks in Tokyo, what might he not see in the eyes of those who survived the leveling and the ash heap of Hiroshima? Yet that part of the country is his family's seat and too close not to visit.

He decided to come bearing sugar, since he knows how badly everyone wants it these days. His team's job is to break up the black markets that have sent prices soaring. The army schools perfected his Japanese. Working in civilian clothes he has confiscated tons of sugar and then watched it disappear from the warehouses, as if through a funnel he is sure leads back into the street.

He came bearing as much as he could pack into one large suitcase, about fifty pounds. But he knew, as soon as he arrived, that he did not need the sugar to cancel out his GI crewcut and his American smile. Being Ko's son was enough, being family. That was all they saw.

They accepted the sugar, of course. But they bowed so graciously, thanking him, you'd scarcely guess their deep craving. Refusing to unwrap the package in his presence, or even seem interested in the contents, they carried it, like a coat in need of a closet, to some other part of the house. Just a hint of embarrassment gave them away, a tinge in the cheek for the fact that such a common item should now be so highly prized. And this was of a piece with their unspoken apology for the general condition of what they had to offer him in return.

Entering, Woody had passed through an immaculate rock garden, its sand white and freshly raked. A hedge of high bamboo bordered it. Inside, the rooms were almost empty—a large, once elegant country house stripped of all but a few mats, an altar in one corner of the first room, a funeral urn. They had not been hit by bombs. The war itself, the years of losing, had turned the house into a clean, swept, airy skeleton.

And yet, if you only watched Aunt Toyo, you might never guess the price of this defeat. She moved with an *ancient, inextinguishable dignity. Her cook prepared for Woody a special meal of teriyaki fish, its sauce enriched by the gift of sugar, and Toyo served it on one of her few remaining treasures, a fine set of porcelain. She served him small, steaming cups of precious prewar sake a cousin had brought along and opened for this celebration. Afterward she led him to a room of clean, close-woven tatami mats and, over his protests, made him accept the thick cover of down-filled silk he's lying under now, a very old and valuable cover by the look and feel of it, so light against him it's like being covered with warm air, and surely the one piece of bedding she has kept for herself.*

His eyes close. How royally they've treated him, he thinks, in spite of all they've lost. How pleased Papa will be to hear of this reception, and to know Toyo is well, and how proud he'll be when Woody returns to tell what a family they come from in Japan. Woody himself is proud already and more than a little relieved to know that those stories Papa used to tell them—about an estate so broad a man could not cross it in one day on horseback, about the generals and the judges and educated women and the fine houses he lived in as a boy—that all those tales were true. Until today, as much as he respects his father, Woody has kept open a little door of doubt. Now that door has softly closed, leaving him wonderfully secure, and stronger, in a room whose dimensions are finally known.

As he dozes, it seems to him a room one can fall asleep in quite easily, a comfortable room, warm, and nearly dark now. He would let the black weight of sleep settle over him completely. But something rouses him. Another presence. Something, or someone has joined him in the room. His eyes spring open.

She is next to him, sitting back on her heels, hands folded in her lap, her dark kimono sheening in the half light, and gazing at him the way she did this afternoon, steadily, intently. This time the tears drop down her cheeks. She had been the one, forty years before, who gave Papa the money he needed to leave Japan and sail to the Hawaiian Islands. His favorite aunt. Her favorite nephew.

Quietly she says, "You look so much like Ko-san. Around the mouth, just like him. And around the eyes. There is a Wakatsuki look, you know, right at the corners, the way the lines crease back."

Involuntarily he reaches up to touch the corner of one eye, feels the wetness there, wants to answer her, wants to find some words to knit those years together, that gap of time. A thickness in his throat makes speech impossible.

She rises. Her eyes drink him in a moment longer. "Sleep. Sleep," she says, and noiselessly scurries out.

He watches her, and watches the screen slide shut, struck by her grace in even this small gesture, learned from centuries of screens slid shut. From somewhere a light illuminates the rich paper texture of the screen. Then the light goes. Woody lies suspended in the warm darkness, buoyed up by a sadness both heavy and sweet. He strokes the skin above his cheekbones, squeezes shut his eyes, to feel what happens when the creases form, tries to visualize it. He rubs his eyes to rub away the water and begins to conjure Papa's face. It takes a long time, as if Papa had to cross the whole Pacific to make his appearance in this room. When he's finally standing there, Woody is amazed at how his stance resembles Toyo's. For the first time he understands that crazy pride. And with his fingertips still touching creases, he marvels at this resemblance too—Papa's eyes, and his own. He'd never seen it *before, never thought to compare himself with Papa, never dared. Now he knows what he should have said while Toyo knelt here.*

"Tell me more about him, Auntie. Tell me how he dressed as a young man, how he walked, and what he did for his amusement. Tell me everything you can remember."

He aches to call her back, and almost does, almost calls her name into the dark, quiet maze of screens and mats and corridors. But doesn't. There is time, he thinks, time for all those questions. Tomorrow we will talk. She likes to recall those days. She says there is still a hill outside of town that Papa used to climb. Tomorrow I will climb it and see what his eyes used to see.

Chapter 19

Re-entry

A few days before we left Manzanar Papa decided that since we *had* to go, we might as well leave in style, and by our own volition. He broke free of the lethargy that had nailed him to our steps for months. He grabbed his Bismarck walking stick and took off, almost at a run, heading for Lone Pine to buy himself a car. Mama tried to talk him out of this. Traveling by bus made much more sense, she said. It was faster, and we'd be there in a day. He snorted with disdain at her advice.

Before the war he had always preferred off-beat, unpredictable cars that no one else of his acquaintance would be likely to own. For a couple of years he drove a long, six-cylinder Chrysler that got about nine miles to the gallon. In the early thirties he drove a Terraplane. Late that afternoon he came back from Lone Pine in a midnight blue Nash sedan, fondling the short, stubby gearshift that projected from its dashboard. The gearshift was what attracted him, and it was one of the few parts of that car to reach southern California unscathed. To get all nine of us, plus our clothes and the odds and ends of furniture we'd accumulated, from Owens Valley 225 miles south to Long Beach, Papa had to make the trip three times. He pushed the car so hard it broke down about every hundred miles or so. In all it took four days.

I went in the first load, with Mama and May and a back seat heaped to the ceiling with dishes and lamps and bedding. A double mattress was tied to the roof. We could have been an Okie family heading west, while Papa in his wide-brim hat and his turtleneck sweater drove like a wild man, as if he couldn't wait to get back to civilization.

I didn't understand this, after all the stories we'd heard. Each time the car collapsed, I prayed we might be stranded there indefinitely. But he could leap out, cursing, and bully it into motion again, fix the tire, replace the fan belt, kick the radiator, whatever was required. I still see him standing by that desert road, in the hot shade of a great saguaro cactus, the blue hood open, as he shouts at the engine in Japanese, damning it and damning the man who sold him this car. He slams the hood shut in disgust, ready to attack it with the butt end of his cane, and that slam, as if by insult, somehow starts the car, so that Papa has to jump in and grab the steering wheel and that dashboard gear knob before the Nash drives away without him.

When he came back from Lone Pine he was drunk, on the first real whiskey he had tasted in years. He was drinking all the way past Mojave, and into the northern suburbs of Los Angeles. There he suddenly sobered up, and his mood began to match what mine had been since we drove out the main gate, as if what we had all been dreading so long was finally to appear, at any moment, without warning—a burst of machine-gun fire, or a row of Burma-Shave signs saying *Japs Go Back Where You Came From.*

The stories, the murmurs, the headlines of the last few months had imprinted in my mind the word hate. I had heard my sisters say, "Why do they hate us?" I had heard Mama say with lonesome resignation, "I don't understand all this hate in the world." It was a bleak and awful-sounding word, yet I had no idea at all what shape it might take if ever I confronted it. I saw it as a dark, amorphous cloud that would descend from above and enclose us forever. As we entered Los Angeles, I sat huddled in the back seat, silent, fearing any word I uttered might bring it to life.

But there was no sign of it anywhere, in fact no response to us at all as we drove down the palm-lined boulevards, past the busy rows of shops and markets, the lawns and driveways of quiet residential streets. Leaving in 1942, no one had any idea what to expect, since no one knew what awaited us; we had been underprepared and that just deepened the shock of what we found. Now the situation was reversed. In our isolated world we had overprepared for shows of abuse. If anything, what greeted us now was indifference. Indeed, if the movements of this city were an indication, the very existence of Manzanar and all it had stood for might be in doubt. The land we drove away from three and a half years earlier had not altered a bit. Here we were, like fleeing refugees, trekking in from some ruined zone of war. And yet, on our six-hour drive south, we seemed to have passed through a time machine, as if, in March of 1942 one had lifted his foot to take a step, had set it down in October of 1945, and was expected just to keep on walking, with all intervening time erased.

In the months to come, because one did have to keep on walking, one desperately wanted to believe nothing had changed during those years of suspended animation. But of course, as we soon discovered, everything had.

Our most immediate problem was where to live. What Papa had read in the papers was true. Housing was short and getting shorter. During 1944 over a million people had moved into California from the south and midwest. But due to wartime priorities, very little new housing had been developed. Now, 60,000 Japanese Americans were returning to their former communities on the west coast and being put into trailer camps, Quonset huts, back rooms of private homes, church social halls, anywhere they could fit.

We were luckier than many. The American Friends Service—the same people who had helped us after the eviction from Terminal Island—helped us rent and move into an apartment in Cabrillo Homes, a housing project in west Long Beach, built by the government for shipyard and defense plant workers. At the time it seemed to be a big step up in the world. There would be no more standing in chow lines; now Mama had a stove to cook on. We had three bedrooms. And we had an inside toilet. As soon as the front door was closed, Papa went in and flushed it, and when it worked, we all hooted with delight.

I didn't really see Cabrillo Homes for what it was until I started high school, a few years later. It looked like a half-finished and undermaintained army base. Long, two-story stucco buildings were set in rows like barracks. Peeling, two-by-four banisters guided you up the outside stairways. Community clotheslines ran above the ragged strips of grass.

Mama picked up the kitchenware and some silver

she had stored with neighbors in Boyle Heights. But the warehouse where she'd stored the rest had been unaccountably "robbed"—of furniture, appliances, and most of those silver anniversary gifts. Papa already knew the car he'd put money on before Pearl Harbor had been repossessed. And, as he suspected, no record of his fishing boats remained. This put him right back where he'd been in 1904, arriving in a new land and starting over from economic zero.

It was another snip of the castrator's scissors, and he never really recovered from this, either financially or spiritually. Yet neither did he entirely give up. One of the amazing things about America is the way it can both undermine you and keep you believing in your own possibilities, pumping you with hope. To maintain some hold on his self-esteem Papa began to pursue his doomed plan for setting up a housing cooperative among the returning Japanese. In our small front room he built a drafting table and worked on sketches for what would become the thick pile of blueprints he carried to households and civic offices all over Los Angeles County, looking for support.

Mama's first concern, meanwhile, as always, was how to keep money coming in. She had saved about $500, but that wouldn't last long. Soon after we settled into Cabrillo Homes, the Friends Service found some openings at one of the fish canneries, and she went back to the kind of job she'd had when we lived on Terminal Island. It meant much more to her now than it had before the war. In 1941, after Papa disappeared, she was marking time while we drifted, awaiting the inevitable. Now she knew the household income was going to be her responsibility for quite a while. Papa would never accept anything like a cannery job. And if he did, Mama's shame would be even greater than his: this would be a sure sign that we had hit rock bottom. So she went to work with as much pride as she could muster. Early each morning she would make up her face. She would fix her hair, cover it with a flimsy net, put on a clean white cannery worker's dress, and stick a brightly colored handkerchief in the lapel pocket. The car pool horn would honk, and she would rush out to join four other Japanese women who had fixed their hair that morning, applied the vanishing cream, and sported freshly ironed hankies.

As for me, the shapeless dread of that great dark cloud in my imagination gradually receded, soothed away by a sky the same blue it had always been, lawns the same green, traffic signals that still changed with dependable regularity, and familiar radio programs to fill up the late afternoons and evenings: *Jack Armstrong, Captain Midnight, The Whistler, I Love a Mystery.* That dread was gone. But those premonitions proved correct, in a way I hadn't been at all prepared for, on the first day back in public school, when the shape of what I truly had to deal with appeared to me for the first time.

Chapter 20

A Double Impulse

When the sixth-grade teacher ushered me in, the other kids inspected me, but not unlike I myself would study a new arrival. She was a warm, benevolent woman who tried to make this first day as easy as possible. She gave me the morning to get the feel of the room. That afternoon, during a reading lesson, she finally asked me if I'd care to try a page out loud. I had not yet opened my mouth, except to smile. When I stood up, everyone turned to watch. Any kid entering a new class wants, first of all, to be liked. This was uppermost in my mind. I smiled wider, then began to read. I made no mistakes. When I finished, a pretty blond girl in front of me said, quite innocently, "Gee, I didn't know you could speak English."

She was genuinely amazed. I was stunned. How could this have even been in doubt?

It isn't difficult, now, to explain her reaction. But at age eleven, I couldn't believe anyone could think such a thing, say such a thing about me, or regard me in that way. I smiled and sat down, suddenly aware of what being of Japanese ancestry was going to be like.

I wouldn't be faced with physical attack, or with overt shows of hatred. Rather, I would be seen as someone foreign, or as someone other than American, or perhaps not be seen at all.

During the years in camp I had never really understood why we were there, nor had I questioned it much. I knew no one in my family had committed a crime. If I needed explanations at all, I conjured up vague notions about a *war* between America and Japan. But now I'd reached an age where certain childhood mysteries begin to make sense. This girl's guileless remark came as an illumination, an instant knowledge that brought with it the first buds of true shame.

From that day on, part of me yearned to be invisible. In a way, nothing would have been nicer than for no one to see me. Although I couldn't have defined it at the time, I felt that if attention were drawn to me, people would see what this girl had first responded to. They wouldn't see me, they would see the slant-eyed face, the Oriental. This is what accounts, in part, for the entire evacuation. You cannot deport 110,000 people unless you have stopped seeing individuals. Of course, for such a thing to happen, there has to be a kind of acquiescence on the part of the victims, some submerged belief that this treatment is deserved, or at least allowable. It's an attitude easy for nonwhites to acquire in America. I had inherited it. Manzanar had confirmed it. And my feeling, at eleven, went something like this: you are going to be invisible anyway, so why not completely disappear.

But another part of me did not want to disappear. With the same sort of reaction that sent Woody into the army, I instinctively decided I would have to prove that I wasn't different, that it should not be odd to hear me speaking English. From that day forward I lived with this double impulse: the urge to disappear and the desperate desire to be acceptable.

I soon learned there were certain areas I was automatically allowed to perform in: scholarship, athletics, and school-time activities like the yearbook, the newspaper, and student government. I tried all of these and made good grades, became news editor, held an office in the Girls Athletic League.

I also learned that outside school another set of rules prevailed. Choosing friends, for instance, often depended upon whether or not I could be invited to their homes, whether their parents would allow this. And what is so infuriating, looking back, is how I accepted the situation. If refused by someone's parents, I would never say, "Go to hell!" or "I'll find other friends," or "Who wants to come to your house anyway?" I would see it as my fault, the result of my failings. I was imposing a burden on *them*.

I would absorb such rejections and keep on looking, because for some reason the scholarship society and the athletic league and the yearbook staff didn't satisfy me, were never quite enough. They were too limited, or too easy, or too obvious. I wanted to declare myself in some different way, and—old enough to be marked by the internment but still too young for the full impact of it to cow me—I wanted *in*.

At one point I thought I would like to join the Girl Scouts. A friend of mine belonged, that blond girl who had commented on my reading. Her name was Radine. Her folks had come west from Amarillo, Texas, and had made a little money in the aircraft plants but not enough yet to get out of Cabrillo Homes. We found ourselves walking partway home together every day. Her fascination with my ability to speak English had led to many other topics. But she had never mentioned the Girl Scouts to me. One day I did.

"Can I belong?" I asked, then adding as an afterthought, as if to ease what I knew her answer would have to be, "You know, I'm Japanese."

"Gee," she said, her friendly face suddenly a mask. "I don't know. But we can sure find out. Mama's the assistant troop leader."

And then, the next day, "Gee, Jeannie, no. I'm *really* sorry."

Rage may have been simmering deep within me, but my conscious reaction was, "Oh well, that's okay, Radine. I understand. I guess I'll see you tomorrow."

"Sure. I'll meet you at the stoplight."

I didn't hold this against her, any more than I associated her personally with the first remark she made. It was her mother who had drawn the line, and I was used to that. If anything, Radine and I were closer now. She felt obliged to protect me. She would catch someone staring at me as we walked home from school and she would growl, "What are *you* looking at? *She's* an American citizen. She's got as much right as anybody to walk around on the street!"

Her outbursts always amazed me. I would much rather have ignored those looks than challenged them. At the same time I wondered why my citizenship had to be so loudly affirmed, and I couldn't imagine why affirming it would really make any difference. (If so, why hadn't it kept me out of Manzanar?) But I was grateful when Radine stuck up for me. Soon we were together all the time. I was teaching her how to twirl baton, and this started a partnership that lasted for the next three years.

I hadn't forgotten what I'd learned in camp. My chubby teacher had taught me well. Radine and I would practice in the grassy plots between the buildings, much as I used to in the firebreaks near Block 28: behind the back, between the legs, over the shoulder, high into the air above the two-story rooftops, watching it, timing its fall for the sudden catch. We practiced the splits, and bending backward, the high-stepping strut, and I saw myself a sequined princess leading orchestras across a football field, the idol of cheering fans.

There happened to be a Boy Scout drum and bugle corps located in the housing project next to ours. They performed in local parades, and they were looking for some baton twirlers to march in front of the band. That fall Radine and I tried out, and we suited them just fine. They made me the lead majorette, in the center between Radine and Gloria, another girl from the seventh grade. Those two wore blue satin outfits to accent their bright blond hair. My outfit was white, with gold braid across the chest. We all wore white, calf-high boots and boat-shaped hats. We worked out trio routines and practiced every weekend with the boys, marching up and down the streets of the project. We performed with them at our junior high assemblies, as well as in the big band reviews each spring, with our batons glinting out in front of the bass drums and snares and shiny bugles, their banners, merit badges, khaki uniforms, and their squared-off military footwork.

This was exactly what I wanted. It also gave me the first sure sign of how certain intangible barriers might be crossed.

The Girl Scouts was much like a sorority, of the kind I would be excluded from in high school and later on in college. And it was run by mothers. The Boy Scouts was like a fraternity and run by fathers. Radine and I were both maturing early. The boys in the band loved having us out there in front of them all the time, bending back and stepping high, in our snug satin outfits and short skirts. Their dads, mostly navy men, loved it too. At that age I was too young to consciously use my sexuality or to understand how an Oriental female can fascinate Caucasian men, and of course far too young to see that even this is usually just another form of invisibility. It simply happened that the attention I first gained as a majorette went hand in hand with a warm reception from the Boy Scouts and their fathers, and from that point on I knew intuitively that one resource I had to overcome the war-distorted limitations of my race would be my femininity.

When Woody came back from Japan, and when Ray came home on leave from the Coast Guard, they would tease me about the short skirts we wore, and about my legs, which were near the other extreme from the heavy-thighed *daikon ashi* of the ballet dancer at Manzanar. They called me *gobo ashi,* after the long, brown, twiglike root vegetable, *gobo.* They laughed. But they would show up for parades whenever they were in town, proud of their neighborhood celebrity.

It was a pride that Papa didn't share. While I was striving to become Miss America of 1947, he was wishing I'd be Miss Hiroshima of 1904. He would counsel me on the female graces, as he understood them, on the need to conceal certain parts of the body, on the gaudiness of smiling too much. But his tastes could not compete with the pull from the world outside our family. For one thing, not much of our family remained. Though larger than the rooms at Manzanar, this apartment was still cramped, forcing us kids outside. We ate in shifts. Mama was gone most of the time. And, worst of all, I had lost respect for Papa. I never dared show this, but it was true.

His scheme for setting up a housing cooperative had failed. With blueprints in hand he tramped through the Japanese community—to hostels, trailer courts, other housing projects like ours—trying to find families who would invest in it. Few had money. Those who did were terrified to let any of it go. And the very idea of banking on some kind of matching support from the government seemed laughable after their internment experience.

Papa needed an enterprise he could manage from within the family. He decided that a fortune could be made catching shrimp and abalone off the coast of Mexico, then bringing it back to dry and sell in southern California. Woody was out of the army by this time and looking for work. As a citizen he could get a commercial license. So at intervals he would rent a boat, take it down to Ensenada or below, load up with abalone, bring the catch home, and all the rest of us would spend days cleaning and cutting up the meat and stringing it out to dry in the bedrooms. For months the apartment reeked of drying seafood.

It was almost a brilliant scheme. In 1947, no one was yet drying abalone commercially. But there was a small worm that kept attacking the drying meat. Papa could never figure out how to control it. This plan too went to pieces.

His failures were sharpened, in an odd way, by Woody's return. He came back from Japan with his mustache thicker and bearing a sword that had been in the family for 300 years—a gift from Aunt Toyo. He brought other trophies, painted scrolls, lacquered trays—things he would have valued only slightly before the war. All of this delighted Papa, filled him with pride for his son who had returned a larger man, with a surer sense of himself and of where we all had come from. Yet while Woody grew, Papa seemed to shrink, losing potency. Their roles had been reversed. Before the war he had been the skipper. Now he depended more and more on Woody, who had youth and a citizen's mobility, who could license the boat or cross borders easily.

Ever more vulnerable, Papa began drinking heavily again. And I would watch it with sorrow and disgust, unable then to imagine what he was going through, too far into my own junior high school survival. I couldn't understand why he was home all day, when Mama had to go out working. I was ashamed of him for that and, in a deeper way, for being what had led to our imprisonment, that is, for being so unalterably Japanese. I would not bring my friends home for fear of what he would say or do.

When he refused to show up for the parades I marched in, this separated me from him that much more, while the events he did show up for left me miserable with embarrassment.

One night the local PTA held an awards dinner for all the students in the scholarship society. I was among them, and this was the sort of achievement Papa encouraged. He and Mama dressed up for the dinner. They overdressed. It was the first time they had mixed socially with Caucasians since leaving camp. Papa seldom spoke to Caucasians during those years, or at any time afterward; when he did it was a point of honor to appear supremely dignified. He still thought of himself as an aristocrat. He bought himself a brand-new single-breasted suit of brown worsted for this occasion, with a matching brown vest and a brown and yellow-flowered silk tie. Mama wore a maroon crepe dress with long sleeves, a necklace of shimmering gold discs, and a black Persian lamb coat I had not seen since before the war. She wore her hair in an upsweep. I knew she felt elegant and glad to be there. She smiled continually, smiled at everyone, as if to make up for Papa's solemn courtesies.

When it came time for each student to be presented a certificate, the parents were introduced. Most of them stood up hastily, or waved from their chairs, like Radine's dad, a big, ruddy Texan, just as unfamiliar with this scene as Papa was. He blushed, grinned foolishly, and everybody grinned back, loving him.

I was standing at the head of the table shaking the principal's hand, when Papa rose, his face ceremoniously grave, and acknowledged the other parents with his most respectful gesture. He pressed his palms together at his chest and gave them a slow, deep, Japanese bow from the waist. They received this with a moment of careful, indecisive silence. He was unforgivably a foreigner then, foreign to them, foreign to me, foreign to everyone but Mama, who sat next to him smiling with pleased modesty. Twelve years old at the time, I wanted to scream. I wanted to slide out of sight under the table and dissolve.

Chapter 21

The Girl of My Dreams

That bow was from the world I wanted out of, while the strutting, sequined partnership I had with Radine was exactly how I wanted my life to go. My path through the next few years can be traced by its relationship to hers. It was a classic situation.

In many ways we had started even. Poor whites from west Texas, her family was so badly off sometimes she'd come to school with no lunch and no money and we would split whatever I had brought along. At the same time we were both getting all this attention together with the drum and bugle corps. After three years at our junior high school, in a ghetto neighborhood that included many Asians, Blacks, Mexicans, and other white migrants from the south, we had ended up close to being social equals.

We stayed best friends until we moved to Long Beach Polytechnic. There everything changed. Our paths diverged. She was asked to join high school sororities. The question of whether or not I should be asked was never even raised. The boys I had crushes on would not ask me out. They would flirt with me in the hallways or meet me after school, but they would ask Radine to the dances, or someone like Radine, someone they could safely be *seen* with. Meanwhile she graduated from baton twirler to song girl, a much more prestigious position in those days. It was unthinkable for a Nisei to be a song girl. Even choosing me as majorette created problems.

The band teacher knew I had more experience than anyone else competing that year. He told me so. But he was afraid to use me. He had to go speak to the board about it, and to some of the parents, to see if it was allowable for an Oriental to represent the high school in such a visible way. It had never happened before. I was told that this inquiry was being made, and my reaction was the same as when I tried to join the Girl Scouts. I was apologetic for imposing such a burden on those who had to decide. When they finally assented, I was grateful. After all, I *was* the first Oriental majorette they'd ever had. Even if my once enviable role now seemed vaguely second-rate, still I determined to try twice as hard to prove they'd made the right choice.

This sort of treatment did not discourage me. I was used to it. I expected it, a condition of life. What demoralized me was watching Radine's success. We had shared everything, including all the values I'd learned from the world I wanted into, not only standards of achievement but ideas about how a girl should look and dress and talk and act, and ideas of male beauty—which was why so many of the boys I liked were Caucasian. Because I so feared never being asked, I often simply made myself unavailable for certain kinds of dates. If one of them had asked, of course, I would have been mortified. That would mean coming to Cabrillo Homes to pick me up, and the very thought of one of his daughters dating a

Caucasian would have started Papa raving. He would have chased the fellow across the grass. This was my dilemma. Easy enough as it was to adopt white American values, I still had a Japanese father to frighten my boyfriends and a Japanese face to thwart my social goals.

I never wanted to change my face or to be someone other than myself. What I wanted was the kind of acceptance that seemed to come so easily to Radine. To this day I have a recurring dream, which fills me each time with a terrible sense of loss and desolation. I see a young, beautifully blond and blue-eyed high school girl moving through a room full of others her own age, much admired by everyone, men and women both, myself included, as I watch through a window. I feel no malice toward this girl. I don't even envy her. Watching, I am simply emptied, and in the dream I want to cry out, because she is something I can never be, some possibility in my life that can never be fulfilled.

It is a schoolgirl's dream, one I tell my waking self I've long since outgrown. Yet it persists. Once or twice a year she will be there, the boyfriend-surrounded queen who passed me by. Surely her example spurred me on to pursue what now seems ludicrous, but at the time was the height of my post-Manzanar ambitions.

It didn't happen in Long Beach. There I felt defeated. I watched Radine's rise, and I knew I could never compete with that. Gradually I lost interest in school and began hanging around on the streets. I would probably have dropped out for good, but it was just about this time that Papa decided to go back into farming and finally moved us out of Cabrillo Homes.

A few months earlier he had almost killed himself on a combination of whiskey and some red wine made by an Italian drinking buddy of his. He had been tippling steadily for two days, when he started vomiting blood from his mouth and nose. It sobered him up permanently. He never touched alcohol again. After that he pulled himself together, and when the chance came along to lease and sharecrop a hundred acres from a big strawberry grower up north in Santa Clara Valley, he took it. That's where he stayed until he died, raising premium berries, outside of San Jose.

I was a senior when we moved. In those days, 1951, San Jose was a large town, but not yet a city. Coming from a big high school in southern California gave me some kind of shine, I suppose. It was a chance to start over, and I made the most of it. By the spring of that year, when it came time to elect the annual carnival queen from the graduating seniors, my homeroom chose me. I was among fifteen girls nominated to walk out for inspection by the assembled student body on voting day.

I knew I couldn't beat the other contestants at their own game, that is, look like a bobbysoxer. Yet neither could I look too Japanese-y. I decided to go exotic, with a flower-print sarong, black hair loose and a hibiscus flower behind my ear. When I walked barefooted out onto the varnished gymnasium floor, between the filled bleachers, the howls and whistles from the boys were double what had greeted any of the other girls. It sounded like some winning basket had just been made in the game against our oldest rivals.

It was pretty clear what the outcome would be, but ballots still had to be cast and counted. The next afternoon I was standing outside my Spanish class when Leonard Rodriguez, who sat next to me, came hurrying down the hall with a revolutionary's fire in his eye. He helped out each day in the administration office. He had just overheard some teachers and a couple of secretaries counting up the votes.

"They're trying to stuff the ballot box," he whispered loudly. "They're fudging on the tally. They're afraid to have a Japanese girl be queen. They've never had one before. They're afraid of what some of the parents will say."

He was pleased he had caught them, and more pleased to be telling this to me, as if some long-held suspicion of conspiracy had finally been confirmed. I shared it with him. Whether this was true or not, I was prepared to believe that teachers would stuff the ballot box to keep me from being queen. For that reason I couldn't afford to get my hopes up.

I said, "So what?"

He leaned toward me eagerly, with final proof. "They want Lois Carson to be queen. I heard them say so."

If applause were any measure, Lois Carson wasn't even in the running. She was too slim and elegant for beauty contests. But her father had contributed a lot to the school. He was on the board of trustees. She was blond, blue-eyed. At that point her name might as well have been Radine. I was ready to capitulate without a groan.

"If she doesn't make carnival queen this year," Leonard went on smugly, "she'll never be queen of anything anywhere else for the rest of her life."

"Let her have it then, if she wants it so much."

"No! We can't do that! *You* can't do that!"

I could do that very easily. I wasn't going to be caught caring about this, or needing it, the way I had needed the majorette position. I already sensed, though I couldn't have said why, that I would lose either way, no matter how it turned out. My face was indifferent.

"How can I stop them from fudging," I said, "if that's what they want to do?"

He hesitated. He looked around. He set his brown face. My champion. "You can't," he said. "But I can."

He turned and hurried away toward the office. The next morning he told me he had gone in there and "raised holy hell," threatened to break this news to the student body and make the whole thing more trouble than it would ever be worth. An hour later the announcement came over the intercom that I had been chosen. I didn't believe it. I couldn't let myself believe it. But, for the classmates who had nominated me, I had to look overjoyed. I glanced across at Leonard and he winked, shouting and whooping now with all the others.

At home that evening, when I brought this news, no one whooped. Papa was furious. I had not told them I was running for queen. There was no use mentioning it until I had something to mention. He asked me what I had worn at the tryouts. I told him.

"No wonder those *hakajin** boys vote for you!" he shouted. "It is just like those majorette clothes you wear in the street. Showing off your body. Is that the kind of queen you want to be?"

I didn't say anything. When Papa lectured, you listened. If anyone spoke up it would be Mama, trying to mediate.

"Ko," she said now, "these things are important to Jeannie. She is . . ."

"Important? I'll tell you what is important. Modesty is important. A graceful body is important. You don't show your legs all the time. You don't walk around like this."

---

*Caucasian.

He did an imitation of a girl's walk, with shoulders straight, an assertive stride, and lips pulled back in a baboon's grin. I started to laugh.

"Don't laugh! This is not funny. You become this kind of woman and what Japanese boy is going to marry you? Tell me that. You put on tight clothes and walk around like Jean Harlow and the *hakajin* boys make you the queen. And pretty soon you end up marrying a *hakajin* boy . . ."

He broke off. He could think of no worse end result. He began to stomp back and forth across the floor, while Mama looked at me cautiously, with a glance that said, "Be patient, wait him out. After he has spoken his piece, you and I can talk sensibly."

He saw this and turned on her. "Hey! How come your daughter is seventeen years old and if you put a sack over her face you couldn't tell she was Japanese from anybody else on the street?"

"Ko," Mama said quietly. "Jeannie's in high school now. Next year she's going to go to college. She's learning other things . . ."

"Listen to me. It's not too late for her to learn Japanese ways of movement. The Buddhist church in San Jose gives odori class twice a week. Jeannie, I want you to phone the teacher and tell her you are going to start taking lessons. Mama has kimonos you can wear. She can show you things too. She used to know all the dances. We have pictures somewhere. Mama, what happened to all those pictures?"

I had seen them, photos of Mama when she lived in Spokane, twelve years old and her round face blanched with rice powder. I remember the afternoon I spent with the incomprehensible old geisha at Manzanar.

"Papa," I complained.

"Don't make faces. You want to be the carnival

queen? I tell you what. I'll make a deal with you. You can be the queen if you start odori lessons at the Buddhist church as soon as school is out."

He stood there, hands on hips, glaring at me, and not at all satisfied with this ultimatum. It was far too late for odori classes to have any effect on me and Papa knew this. But he owed it to himself to make one more show of resistance. When I signed up, a few weeks later, I lasted about ten lessons. The teacher herself sent me away. I smiled too much and couldn't break the habit. Like a majorette before the ever-shifting sidewalk crowd, I smiled during performances, and in Japanese dancing that is equivalent to a concert violinist walking onstage in a bathing suit.

Papa didn't mention my queenship again. He just glared at me from time to time, with great distaste, as if I had betrayed him. Yet in that glare I sometimes detected a flicker of approval, as if this streak of independence, this refusal to be shaped by him reflected his own obstinance. At least, these glances seemed to say, she has inherited *that*.

Mama, of course, was very proud. She took charge and helped me pick out the dress I would wear for the coronation. We drove to San Jose and spent an afternoon in the shops downtown. She could take time for such things now that Papa was working again. This was one of the few days she and I ever spent together, just the two of us, and it confirmed something I'd felt since early childhood. In her quiet way, she had always supported me, alongside of or underneath Papa's demands and expectations. Now she wanted for me the same thing I thought I wanted. Acceptance, in her eyes, was simply another means for survival.

Her support and Papa's resistance had one point in common: too much exposure was unbecoming. All the other girls—my four attendants—were going strapless. Mama wouldn't allow this. By the time we finished shopping, I had begun to agree with her. When she picked out a frilly ball gown that covered almost everything and buried my legs under layers of ruffles, I thought it was absolutely right. I had used a low-cut sarong to win the contest. But once chosen I would be a white-gowned figure out of *Gone With the Wind;* I would be respectable.

On coronation night the gym was lit like a church, with bleachers in half-dark and a throne at one end, flooded brightly from the ceiling. The throne was made of plywood, its back shaped in a fleur-de-lis all covered with purple taffeta that shone like oily water under moonlight. Bed sheets were spread to simulate a wide, white carpet the length of the gym, from the throne of the door of the girls' locker room where, with my attendants, we waited for the PA system to give us our musical cue.

Lois Carson, the trustee's daughter, was one of them. She wore a very expensive strapless gown and a huge orchid corsage. Her pool-browned shoulders glowed in the harsh bulb light above the lockers.

"Oh Jeannie," she had said, as we took off our coats. "What a marvelous idea!"

I looked at her inquisitively.

"The high *neck*," she explained, studying my dress. "You look so . . . *sedate*. Just perfect for a queen."

As the other girls arrived, she made sure they all agreed with this. "Don't you *wish* you'd thought of it," she would say. And then to me, during a silence she felt obliged to fill, "I just *love* Chinese food." The others exclaimed that they too loved Chinese food, and we talked about recipes and restaurants until the music faded in:

> *Girl of my dreams, I love you,*
> *Honest I do,*
> *You are so sweet.*

It swelled during the opening bars to cover all other sounds in the gym. I stepped out into blue light that covered the first sheet, walking very slowly, like you do at weddings, carrying against the white bodice of my gown a bouquet of pink carnations.

A burst of applause resounded beneath the music, politely enthusiastic, followed by a steady murmur. The gym was packed, and the lights were intense. Suddenly it was too hot out there. I imagined that they were all murmuring about my dress. They saw the girls behind me staring at it. The throne seemed blocks away, and now the dress was stifling me. I had never before worn such an outfit. It was not at all what I should have on. I wanted my sarong. But then thought, no. That would have been worse. Papa had been right about the sarong. Maybe he was right about everything. What was I doing out there anyway, trying to be a carnival queen? The teachers who'd counted the votes certainly didn't think it was such a good idea. Neither did the trustees. The students wanted me though. Their votes proved that. I kept walking my processional walk, thinking of all the kids who had voted for me, not wanting to let them down, although in a way I already had. It wasn't the girl in this old-fashioned dress they had voted for. But if not her, who *had* they voted for? Somebody I wanted to be. And wasn't. Who was I then? According to the big wall speakers now saxophoning through the gym, I was the girl of somebody's dream:

> *Since you've been gone, dear,*
> *Life don't seem the same.*
> *Please come back again . . .*

I looked ahead at the throne. It was even further away, a purple carriage receding as I approached. I glanced back. My four attendants seemed tiny. Had they stopped back there? Afterward there would be a little reception in one of the classrooms, punch and cookies under flourescent tubes. Later, at Lois Carson's house, there'd be a more intimate, less public gathering, which I'd overheard a mention of but wouldn't be invited to. Champagne in the foothills. Oyster dip. I wanted to laugh. I wanted to cry. I wanted to be ten years old again, so I could believe in princesses and queens. It was too late. Too late to be an odori dancer for Papa, too late to be this kind of heroine. I wanted the carnival to end so I could go somewhere private, climb out of my stuffy dress, and cool off. But all eyes were on me. It was too late now not to follow this make-believe carpet to its plywood finale, and I did not yet know of any truer destination.

Mountain snow loosens rivulets of tears.
Washed stones, forgotten clearing.

J.W.H.

PART THREE

PART THREE

Chapter 22

Ten Thousand Voices

As I came to understand what Manzanar had meant, it gradually filled me with shame for being a person guilty of something enormous enough to deserve that kind of treatment. In order to please my accusers, I tried, for the first few years after our release, to become someone acceptable. I both succeeded and failed. By the age of seventeen I knew that *making it*, in the terms I had tried to adopt, was not only unlikely, but false and empty, no more authentic for me than trying to emulate my Great-aunt Toyo. I needed some grounding of my own, such as Woody had found when he went to commune with her and with our ancestors in Ka-ke. It took me another twenty years to accumulate the confidence to deal with what the equivalent experience would have to be for me.

It's outside the scope of this book to recount all that happened in the interim. Suffice to say, I was the first member of our family to finish college and the first to marry out of my race. As my husband and I began to raise our family, and as I sought for ways to live agreeably in Anglo-American society, my memories of Manzanar, for many years, lived far below the surface. When we finally started to talk about making a trip to visit the ruins of the camp, something would inevitably get in the way of our plans. Mainly my own doubts, my fears. I half-suspected that the place did not exist. So few people I met in those years had even heard of it, and those who had knew so little about it, sometimes I imagined I had made the whole thing up, dreamed it. Even among my brothers and sisters, we seldom discussed the internment. If we spoke of it at all, we joked.

When I think of how that secret lived in all our lives, I remember the way Kiyo and I responded to a little incident soon after we got out of camp. We were sitting on a bus-stop bench in Long Beach, when an old, embittered woman stopped and said, "Why don't all you dirty Japs go back to Japan!" She spit at us and passed on. We said nothing at the time. After she stalked off down the sidewalk we did not look at each other. We sat there for maybe fifteen minutes with downcast eyes and finally got up and walked home. We couldn't bear to mention it to anyone in the family. And over the years we never spoke of this insult. It stayed alive in our separate memories, but it was too painful to call out into the open.

In 1966 I met a Caucasian woman who had worked for one year as a photographer at Manzanar. I could scarcely speak to her. I desperately wanted to, but all my questions stuck in my throat. This time it was not the pain of memory. It was simply her validation that all those things had taken place. Someone outside the close community of Japanese Americans had actually seen the camp, with its multitude of people and its swarm of buildings on the plain between the mountains. Something inside me opened then. I began to talk about it more and more.

It was April 1972, thirty years almost to the day, that we piled our three kids into the car and headed out there. From where we live now, in the California coast town of Santa Cruz, it's a full day's drive. We started down 101 to Paso Robles, crossed over the hummocky Diablo Range to the central valley, skirted Bakersfield, and climbed through Tehachapi Pass into the desert.

At Mojave we turned north onto the same road our bus had taken out from Los Angeles in April 1942. It is the back road to the Sierras and the main route from southern California to Reno and Lake Tahoe. We joined bikers and backpackers and the skiers heading for Mammoth. The traffic through there is fast, everyone but the bikers making for the high country. As we sped along wide roads at sixty and seventy, with our kids exclaiming at the sights we passed and our car loaded down with camping gear, it seemed even more incredible to me that a place like Manzanar could have been anywhere within reach of such a highway, such a caravan of pleasure-seeking travelers.

The bikers peeled off at Red Rock Canyon, a gorgeous bulge of pink cliffs and rusty gulches humping out of the flatlands. After that it was lovely desert but nothing much to stop for. In a hundred miles we passed two oases, the first at Olancha, the second around Lone Pine, a small, tree-filled town where a lot of mountain buffs turn off for the Mount Whitney Portal.

A few miles out of Lone Pine we started looking for another stand of trees, some tall elms, and what remains of those gnarled pear orchards. They were easy to spot. Everything else is sagebrush, tumble-weeds, and wind.

At its peak, in the summer of '42, Manzanar was the biggest city between Reno and Los Angeles, a special kind of western boom town that sprang from the sand, flourished, had its day, and now has all but disappeared. The barracks are gone, torn down right after the war. The guard towers are gone, and the mess halls and shower rooms, the hospital, the tea gardens, and the white buildings outside the compound. Even the dust is gone. Spreading brush holds it to the ground. Thirty years earlier, army bulldozers had scraped everything clean to start construction.

What you see from the road are the two gatehouses, each a small empty pillbox of a building faced with flagstones and topped, like tiny pagodas, with shingled curving roofs. Farther in, you see the elms, most of which were planted by internees, and off to the right a large green building that was once our high school auditorium, now a maintenance depot for the Los Angles Power and Water District, who leased the land to the government during the war and still owns it.

Past the gatehouses we turned left over a cattle guard and onto a dirt perimeter road that led to the far side of the campsite. About half a mile in we spotted a white obelisk gleaming in the distance and marking a subtle line where the plain begins gradually to slope upward into the alluvial fan that becomes the base of the mountains. It seemed miraculous, as if some block of stone had fallen from the peaks above and landed upright in the brush, chiseled, solitary, twelve feet high.

Near it a dozen graves were outlined in the sand with small stones, and a barbed-wire fence sur-rounded them to keep back the cattle and the tumbleweed. The black Japanese script cut into the white face of the obelisk read simply, "A Memorial to the Dead."

We were alone out there, too far from the road to hear anything but wind. I thought of Mama, now seven years gone. For a long time I stood gazing at the monument. I couldn't step inside the fence. I believe in ghosts and spirits. I knew I was in the presence of those who had died at Manzanar. I also felt the spiritual presence that always lingers near awesome wonders like Mount Whitney. Then, as if rising from the ground around us on the valley floor, I began to here the first whispers, nearly inaudible, from all those thousands who once had lived out here, a wide, windy sound of the ghost of that life. As we began to walk, it grew to a murmur, a thin steady hum.

We turned the kids loose, watched them scamper off ahead of us, and we followed what used to be an asphalt road running from the back side of the camp a mile out to the highway. The obelisk—built in 1943—and the gatehouses are all that have survived intact from internment days. The rest of the place looks devastated by a bombing raid.

The old road was disintegrating, split, weed-sprung. We poked through the remains of hospital foundations, undermined by erosion channels. We found concrete slabs where the latrines and shower rooms stood, and irrigation ditches, and here and there, the small rock arrangements that once decorated many of the entranceways. I had found out that even in North Dakota, when Papa and the other Issei men imprisoned there had free time, they would gather small stones from the plain and spend hours sorting through a dry stream bed looking for the veined or polished rock that somehow pleased the most. It is so characteristically Japanese, the way lives were made more tolerable by gathering loose desert stones and forming with them something enduringly human. These rock gardens had outlived the barracks and the towers and would surely outlive the asphalt road and rusted pipes and shattered slabs of concrete. Each stone was a mouth, speaking for a family, for some man who had beautified his doorstep.

Vegetation gets thickest toward the center of the site, where the judo pavilion once stood and where rows of elms planted as windbreaks have tripled their growth since the forties. In there we came across the remains of a small park. A stone-lined path ran along the base of a broad mound of dirt about five feet high. Stones had been arranged on the mound, and some low trees still shaded it and made an arch above the path. For a moment I was strolling again, finding childish comfort in its incongruous design.

But after ten feet the path ended in tumbleweeds. The trees were dry and stubby, the mound was barren, and my attention was arrested by a water faucet sticking two feet out of the sand, like some subterranean periscope. One of these had provided water for each barracks. They stuck up at intervals in every direction, strangely sharpening the loneliness and desolation, sometimes the only sign of human presence in an acre or two of sand.

My mood had shifted. The murmur turned to wind. For a while I could almost detach myself from the place and its history and take pleasure in it purely as an archaeological site. I saw the outlines, patterns this city must have taken. I imagined where the buildings stood, almost as I once did nosing around old Roman villas in Europe. We saw a low ring of stones built up with cement and wondered who the mason was who knelt there and studied the shapes before fitting them together. We moved around the ring a few feet to find out. This was the old flagpole circle, where the Stars and Stripes were hoisted every morning, and the inscription scratched across the top said, BUILT BY WADA AND CREW, JUNE 10, 1942 A.D.

The A.D. made me shiver. I knew that the man who inscribed it had foreseen these ruins and did not want his masonry identified with the wrong era. His words coming out of the stone became a voice that merged with all the others, not a murmur this time, but low voices muttering and chattering all around me. We were crossing what used to be a firebreak, now a sandy field devoid of any growth. The wind was vicious there, with nothing to break it, and the voices grew. The firebreak was where we had talent shows and dances and outdoor movies in the summer, and where the kids played games. I heard the girls' glee club I used to sing in, way off from the other side of camp, their tiny grade-school sopranos singing, "Beautiful dreamer, wake unto me." I closed my eyes and I was ten years old again. Nothing had changed. I heard laughter. It was almost dusk, the wind had dropped, and I saw old men squatting in the dirt, Papa and some of his cronies, muttering and smoking their cigarettes. In the summertime they used to burn orange peels under gallon cans, with holes punched in the sides, to keep the mosquitoes away. Sometimes they would bring out their boards to play *goh* and *hana*. The orange peels would smolder in there, and the men would hunker down around the cans and watch the smoke seep out the holes.

From that firebreak we cut across toward the first row of pear trees, looking for what might remain of Block 28. There wasn't much to guide us but the trees themselves and a view I remembered of the blunt, bulky Inyo Range that bounds the eastern limit of the valley. When we were close enough to smell the trees we stopped. They were stunted, tenacious, tough, the way a cactus has to be. The water table in that one area has kept them living through all these years of neglect, and they were ready to bloom at any moment. The heady smell was as odd in that desert setting as the little scrap of park had been, as odd yet just as familiar. We used to picnic there in blossom time, on weekends, if we got a wind-free day.

The wind blew it toward us now—chilled pear nectar—and it blew our kids around a high stand of brush. They came tumbling across the sand, demanding to know what we were going to *do* out here. Our twins were five years old at the time, a boy and a girl. Our older daughter had just turned eleven. She knew about "the evacuation," but it would be a few more years before she absorbed this part of the family history. For these three the site had been like any wreck or ruin. They became explorers, rushed around hoping the next clump of dusty trees or chunk of wall might reveal the treasure, the trinket, the exotically rusted hinge. Nothing much had turned up. The shine was wearing off the trip. Their eyes were red and their faces badly chapped. No place for kids.

My husband started walking them back to the car. I stayed behind a moment longer, first watching our eleven-year-old stride ahead, leading her brother and sister. She has long dark hair like mine and was then the same age I had been when the camp closed. It was so simple, watching her, to see why everything that had happened to me since we left camp referred back to it, in one way or another. At that age your body is changing, your imagination is galloping, your mind is in that zone between a child's vision and an adult's. Papa's life ended at Manzanar, though he lived for twelve more years after getting out. Until this trip I had not been able to admit that my own life really began there. The times I thought I had dreamed it were one way of getting rid of it, part of wanting to lose it, part of what you might call a whole Manzanar mentality I had lived with for twenty-five years. Much more than a remembered place, it had become a state of mind. Now, having seen it, I no longer wanted to lose it or to have those years erased. Having found it, I could say what you can only say when you've truly come to know a place: Farewell.

I had nearly outgrown the shame and the guilt and the sense of unworthiness. This visit, this pilgrimage, made comprehensible, finally, the traces that remained and would always remain, like a needle. That hollow ache I carried during the early months of internment had shrunk, over the years, to a tiny sliver of suspicion about the very person I was. It had grown so small sometimes I'd forget it was there. Months might pass before something would remind me. When I first read, in the summer of 1972, about the pressure Japan's economy was putting on American business and how a union in New York City had printed up posters of an American flag with MADE IN JAPAN written across it, then that needle began to jab. I heard Mama's soft, weary voice from 1945 say, "It's all starting over." I knew it wouldn't. Yet neither would I have been surprised to find the FBI at my door again. I would resist it much more than my parents did, but deep within me something had been prepared for that. Manzanar would always live in my nervous system, a needle with Mama's voice.

A gust of wind rushed through the orchard, bringing ice off the white slopes, and more blossom scent. It hurt to inhale deeply. I pulled my coat tight, ready to head for the car's warmth, but also wanting to hold this moment a little longer. I might never be back here again. I was poking around brush clumps and foundation chunks looking for something else. One more sign. Anything. I found another collection of stones, off by themselves, but so arranged that they could not have been accidental. Nearby an edge showed through the sand. I uncovered a single steppingstone, slightly worn, that led nowhere, yet lay as a subtle appendage to the small rock garden. One of these had lain outside our barracks door, a first step below three wooden ones. It could be ours. Perhaps not. Many barracks had such entrances. But this one would serve. I could call it the rock garden Papa put there. Almost the sign I wanted. Not quite. Not quite enough. There was more to all this than the lovely patience of these gathered stones. They were part of it. But there was something else, in the air. A sound. A smell. Just a whiff, hanging on that gust from the orchard, or blown down the ghostly alleyway of what used to be the street we lived on. I was hearing Mama's voice once more, but differently, louder now, right in front of me, and I smelled cork burning. That was one of Papa's remedies when her back knotted up. He would take little coins of cork and place them on the tension nodes and light them, and the cork would burn dark rings into her skin as she hunched on the porch steps groaning with relief.

They were sitting on the steps like that—Mama hunched, Papa tending the blackening rings—one morning a few days before we left camp. Now that smell and those voices in the wind from the orchard brought with them the sign I was waiting for: the image of a rekindled wildness in Papa's eyes. Twenty-seven years earlier I had carried it with me out of camp only half understanding what it meant.

Remembering now, I realized I had never forgotten his final outburst of defiance. But for the first time I saw it clearly, as clearly as the gathered desert stones, and when I left today for good I would carry that image with me again, as the rest of my inheritance.

It was the day Papa suddenly came back to life and decided to go into Lone Pine and buy a car. Mama had been packing, and that brought the uncertainty of our future to such a sharp point, her back went into spasms. She didn't want to talk. She wanted to concentrate on the rings of heat. She let Papa rant a long time before she reacted.

"That's crazy, Ko," she said.

"Don't call me crazy! You think I'm going to ride that stinking bus all the way to Los Angeles?"

"It's cheaper than buying a car."

"Cheaper! What is it worth—to be packed in there like cattle? You call that cheap?"

"We don't have money to buy a car."

"I know how much money we have!"

He jumped to his feet then, rushed into the house, came out with his hat on and a shirt half-buttoned, and his walking stick and his turtleneck sweater tied around his neck, and took off striding toward the main gate, leaving Mama with her back full of smoking cork, which had done no good at all, since this new move of his merely bunched her muscles up worse than ever.

It was late afternoon when we heard the horn, still blocks away. Without looking out the door, Mama said, "Here he comes."

As the honks came closer we heard another sound, like a boxer working out a flabby punching bag. Mama moved to the doorway. We all did—Chizu, May, me—in time to see a blue Nash four-door come around the corner, with its two front tires flat and Papa sitting up straight and proud behind the wheel, his hat cocked, his free hand punching at the horn. Heads were appearing at doorways all up and down the street.

He stopped in front, racing the engine and grinning, while he eyed Mama and fingered the shiny-knobbed dashboard gearshift. On the seat between his legs he held a half-empty quart bottle of whiskey. He yelled, "What do you think, Little Mama?"

She didn't answer. He had not been drinking much at all for about six months. She stood there waiting to see what he was going to do. He laughed and made the engine roar and demanded to know where all his boys were, he wanted to show those *yogores* what a real car looked like. Kiyo was the only son still in camp, and he had gone off to help someone else load furniture. So Papa announced that he would give all his women a ride. Mama protested, said he ought to get those tires fixed if we expected to take this car all the way into Los Angeles. Papa roared back at her, louder than the engine, and with such a terrible samurai's scowl that we all went leaping and piling into the car, Mama last, slamming the back door and climbing into the front seat next to him.

"You think it's a pretty good car?" he said, pleased by this show of power.

Mama said nothing. She sat very stiff, cool, enduring him.

Chizu was the placator now, leaning forward from the back to pat him on the shoulder. "It's a fine car, papa."

"You watch!"

He grabbed the gear lever and rammed it into low. The Nash leaped, and we were cloppeting down the street on those two flats and two good tires, with Papa laughing, sipping from the bottle. At the first corner he said, "You think I can't pick out cars?"

Softly Chizu said, "You did real good, Papa."

He stepped on the gas, hitting maybe thirty, swerving crazily. In the back seat we were all thrown around, flung from door to door like rag dolls, with mama bouncing in front of us and papa's hat crunching up against the ceiling.

May cried out, "Not so fast, Papa! You're going to wreck your car!"

"Think the car can't take it?" he yelled back at her. "You watch this!"

His gaiety turned ferocious again. He stomped the pedal, pushing the speedometer up to thirty-five. His right front tire had shredded and it flopped like a mangled arm. It lashed out, upending a garbage can. I started to cry. Chizu, her calm shattered, was yelling at him to slow down, Mama was too, and May was screaming. He wouldn't listen and told us to hold on, while he swung into the street, careening past emptying barracks where suitcases and duffel bags sat stacked. As we passed people standing by the baggage, Papa swerved from one side to the other, waving. He laughed, growled, made faces. In front of us, a laden family was hiking out toward the main gate. Papa swung wide, honking, and waving.

"Hey! Hey!" he shouted.

They turned, too amazed to wave back.

"Don't miss that bus!" he yelled.

At the next corner he spun off into a deserted section of barracks. These already looked like the ones we'd first moved into, sand piling up against foundation blocks, the clotheslines empty, all signs and markers gone. It made no difference to Papa that no one was out there to witness his performance. He aimed for tumbleweeds lying in the roadbed and shouted with triumph each time he squashed one. Chizu and Mama and May had quit trying to control him. I'd stopped crying. We grabbed for handholds, covered our heads, hoping simply to survive until he hit something hard or ran out of gas.

We came to a firebreak and Papa plunged into it, began to cut a twisty path across its emptiness, shouting "Hyah! Hyah!," gouging ragged tracks through the dusty sand. The way this firebreak lay, there seemed to be nothing in front of us now but sagebrush and open country, rising in the distance south of camp to the range of round, buff-colored hills rumored to be full of rattlesnakes. The few times I'd wished I could walk in one direction for as long as I wanted, the threat of those rattlesnakes deterred me. And now, farther south, beyond that visible barrier, out in the world I scarcely remembered, there loomed the dark, threatening cloud I'd heard grown-ups talk about. The way we seemed to be heading, I should have been frightened into a coma. But for this once, I was not. Watching Papa bounce and weave and shout in front of me, I was almost ready to laugh with him, with the first bubbly sense of liberation his defiant craziness had brought along with it. I believed in him completely just then, believed in the fierceness flashing in his wild eyes. Somehow that would get us past whatever waited inside the fearful dark cloud, get us past the heat, and the rattlers, and a great deal more.

At the fence he had to turn, sending up a white billow of dust. Where the fence met the highway we cornered again, heading for the bus stop. A crowd waited there, standing idly, sitting around on scattered baggage. They all turned to watch when they heard us coming. Papa tooted the horn and yelled out, "No bus for us! No bus for us!"

The young kids were mystified by this and stood open-eyed, watching. Some of the older folks smiled, waving as we hit a chuck hole and bounced. Papa swung left, and we clattered out onto the wide, empty boulevard that ran the length of the camp, back to where our own baggage waited and the final packing.

Related Readings

CONTENTS

from **Legends from Camp**
poems by Lawson Fusao Inada

The Legend of Superman
Some things even Superman
doesn't understand. 179

The Legend of Home
Home seems so far away. 180

Sleep in the Mojave Desert
An inhospitable place to rest
poem by Sylvia Plath 182

I Remember Pearl Harbor: Dealing
with the "Problem Race"
Why the nation should apologize
to interned Japanese Americans
essay by Charles Shiro Inouye 184

Wilshire Bus
A former internee's surprising
reaction to anti-Chinese prejudice
short story by Hisaye Yamamoto 191

Trains at Night
> *In 1930s Mexico, all Chinese are*
> *ordered out, but Mr. Lee finds a place*
> *to hide.*
> **short story** by Alberto Alvaro Ríos   198

Visiting Home
> *An African-American family is*
> *displaced from their Louisiana farm.*
> **poem** by Kevin Young   208

***from* Unto the Sons**
> *What was it like to grow up Italian-*
> *American during World War II?*
> **memoir** by Gay Talese   212

**Lectures on How You Never Lived
Back Home**
> *A multiple identity: smart American*
> *girl, beautiful Filipina, dutiful*
> *daughter*
> **short story** by M. Evelina Galang   221

from Legends from Camp

by Lawson Fusao Inada

Following are 2 poems from a series of 25 poems based on the writer's boyhood memories of the Jerome internment camp in Arkansas and the Amache camp in Colorado. What more do these poems tell you about the internment's effects on children?

XVIII. THE LEGEND OF SUPERMAN

Superman, being Superman,
had his headquarters out there
somewhere between Gotham City
and Battle Creek, Michigan.

5   Superman, being Superman,
even knew my address:

      Block 6G, 5 C
      Amache, Colorado
      America

10   And Superman, being Superman,
sent me his Secret Code,
based on all the Planets—

with explicit instructions
to keep it hidden from others,

15 like "under a bed, a sofa,
    or under stockings in a drawer."

    Superman, being Superman,
    didn't seem to understand.
    Where could anything hide?

20 And, since we all spoke code
    on a regular basis, day to day,

    Superman, being Superman,
    gathered up his Planets
    and simply flew away!

XX. THE LEGEND OF HOME

    Home, too, was out there.
    It had names like
    Marysville, Placerville,
    Watsonville, and Lodi—

5   and they were all big cities,
    or at least bigger than camp.

    And they were full of trees,
    and grass, with fruit
    for the picking, dogs
10 to chase, cats to catch

    on streets and roads
    where Joey and Judy lived.

    Imagine that!
    The blue tricycle

15   left in the weeds somewhere!
     And when you came to a fence,
     you went around it!

     And one of those homes
     not only had a tunnel
20   but an overpass
     that, when you went over,

     revealed everything
     going on forever up to
     a gleaming bridge
25   leading into neon lights
     and ice cream leaning
     double-decker.

     Imagine that!

Sleep in the Mojave Desert

by Sylvia Plath

Manzanar was near the Mojave Desert,
which spans California and Nevada. The
speaker in this poem, like the residents of
Manzanar, finds that the desert offers no
welcome.

Out here there are no hearthstones,
Hot grains, simply. It is dry, dry.
And the air dangerous. Noonday acts queerly
On the mind's eye, erecting a line
5   Of poplars in the middle distance, the only
Object beside the mad, straight road
One can remember men and houses by.
A cool wind should inhabit those leaves
And a dew collect on them, dearer than
    money,
10   In the blue hour before sunup.
Yet they recede, untouchable as tomorrow,
Or those glittery fictions of spilt water
That glide ahead of the very thirsty.

I think of the lizards airing their tongues
15   In the crevice of an extremely small shadow
And the toad guarding his heart's droplet.
The desert is white as a blind man's eye,
Comfortless as salt. Snake and bird
Doze behind the old masks of fury.

20   We swelter like firedogs in the wind.
The sun puts its cinder out. Where we lie
The heat-cracked crickets congregate
In their black armorplate and cry.
The day-moon lights up like a sorry mother,
25   And the crickets come creeping into our hair
To fiddle the short night away.

I Remember Pearl Harbor: Dealing with the "Problem Race"

by Charles Shirō Inouye

This essay discusses the bill, made law in 1988, that offered a national apology to Japanese Americans interned during the war and authorized a payment of $20,000 to each surviving internee. Find out why the writer considers this bill "an important milestone in our journey as a nation."

Franklin D. Roosevelt called the Japanese attack on Pearl Harbor forty-seven years ago "a day that will live in infamy," but infamy is hard to gauge. We are a nation of many peoples, and international insult is not always uniformly felt. December 7, 1941, was a fateful day for my own family. But perhaps more infamous was February 19, 1942, when President Roosevelt, a man who had posed as the immigrant's friend and as a leader with a vision of a fairer America, signed Executive Order 9066. That order eventually set apart Washington, Oregon, the western half of California and the southern third of Arizona as areas from which all persons of Japanese ancestry were to be removed. That included my father, who was living in Menlo Park, California, and my mother, who was living in Yakima, Washington. They were sent to live in a relocation camp in Wyoming.

They were both citizens of the United States and thus guaranteed certain rights by the Constitution. Their right to address the decision that would uproot them from their homes, for example, was actually honored by the creation of a forum in which all Japanese-Americans were invited to participate. These were the so-called Tolan hearings, headed by Representative John Tolan of California. This public debate on the evacuation question began on February 21, 1942, and ended on March 12. The 980-page report of the hearings eloquently describes a travesty. Set against the testimony of the military experts and those of other pro-evacuation groups (who for three decades had found a voice in the newspapers of William Randolph Hearst), the voice of my grandfather's people is weak and pitiful.

The *issei,* or first generation immigrants, not only spoke English poorly but also, having lived in segregated farming and fishing communities, had little experience as debaters. Their children, the *nisei,* had attended public schools and frequently became valedictorians and salutatorians in their pursuit of the American dream; but they were simply too young to protect themselves in such a hostile arena. What the decision-making process that led to the evacuation tells us is that an offer to participate in the democratic process does not necessarily insure justice. Invited to dine at the fox's home, the heron ate poorly.

This is not to say that the forum made no difference. It did. Study the arguments of those who were in favor of the evacuation and you will find an interesting shift in strategy. At first, the crux of this modest proposal to remove tens of thousands of ethnic Japanese from their homes and put them in concentration camps built in the outback of America was that the non-Japanese on the West Coast must be protected from invasion. The Army claimed that the Japanese immigrants were signaling submarines off the coast, secretly participating in other deeds of sabotage and, therefore, had to be sent somewhere else. (My mother, for instance, who had taken a job as a live-in maid for a dentist in Seattle, was interrogated by the Federal Bureau of Investigation because her bedroom window overlooked Puget Sound.) Though many such accusations were made, none were substantiated. Later, retreating from their obviously racist position, proponents of evacuation formed an argument that was at least outwardly more benign: The government of the United States must act quickly in order to protect Japanese immigrants from the whites who were seeking to harm them.

Now things were switched around—the mouse was chasing the cat. But whatever the case, this burden of protection that the military took upon itself (despite objections from the Justice Department) presupposed an insidious form of inequality. As the history of blacks and Native Americans in the United States also demonstrates, governmental protection is, for all its comforting rhetoric, too often a denial of justice and dignity. It requires restrictions of liberty and asks that the "problem race" be grateful for the many favors extended to it. Those favors would in the case of the Japanese include, to quote the stone and brass historical marker that graces what remains of the Heart Mountain camp in Wyoming, "first-class schools, electricity and plumbing."

Last summer, forty-six years after the fact, President Reagan signed HR 442, a bill to redress the wartime internment of Japanese-American civilians. This acknowledges the injustice of Roosevelt's act and stands as a national apology and as a tax break to those evacuees still alive. I separate the apology from the stipend because that is how the survivors of the evacuation see it. What does $20,000, to be paid over a ten-year period, mean to people who were forced from their homes by hysterical overreaction? The money is a pittance, one my parents never expected to receive and one that will give them little joy. (There is talk about pooling the money to establish scholarship funds for the needy, and to create research grants for the study of Japanese-American history.)

But the apology really matters. The bill may be essentially an attempt at restitution, but it should not be understood as something designed to restore dignity to the Japanese-Americans. While it is undeniable that the *nisei* have been fighting to regain face ever since Roosevelt's order, in truth they never lost their self-respect. Along with one suitcase of personal effects, dignity was something everyone took with them to the camps. The evacuation did not disgrace those who went but those who sent them.

The point is that if patriotism and the Pledge of Allegiance can be revived as unifying national concerns, as George Bush deployed them in the recent campaign, then so must dignity and the ability to apologize for our mistakes. This is why HR 442 is an important milestone in our journey as a nation. By seeing that justice is done, HR 442 restores our commitment to the belief that all people deserve to be treated well. As an affirmation of civil rights, this act makes all Americans a bit more humane because it admits that we as a group can make mistakes, that we can be contrite and that we can do something about our errors. Finally, the bill is important because it raises the issue of a national apology and brings into focus the relationship of the individual to the state in a way that no amount of flag-waving can.

As brilliant as fireworks may be, we can only see ourselves clearly in light that is more focused and steady. Too bad, then, that for every well-developed thought about the real state of our union there are a hundred empty slogans and a million statements of self-congratulation. Rare are the moments when nations are forced to think about themselves in something other than a celebratory or a defensive way. Japan's unconditional surrender to the Allied forces was, to bring in a relevant point of comparison, one of these rare moments. As Emperor Hirohito spoke to his people, he renounced his own divinity; and by this act the symbols and institutions that had brought a nation together to wage war suddenly lost authority. This was precisely what the United States sought. Our country, the victor, saw state Shinto as an abomination; and, after dropping nuclear bombs on two of Japan's cities, we forced a spiritual apology in order to plant the seeds of pluralism in the scorched wasteland of the Japanese soul.

What most Americans fail to realize is that the vast majority of Japanese actually do regret having fought the war. They regret it more profoundly than we, who, ironically, are now asking them to remilitarize. Led by the belief that they were a chosen and blessed nation, they engaged in a program of destruction and bloodshed that left much of East Asia in ashes. It was a hellish experience; and the remorse felt by some segments of the population is still so intense that the museums erected to the memory of Hiroshima and Nagasaki have been carefully denuded of any sign of politics, lest they become rallying points for partisans who would interfere with the orderly building of the new and improved Japan.

Consequently, the message we get as we walk past the photographs of melted buildings and torn flesh in the Hiroshima display is that science has created a terrible device, and that the device, not the people who design and use it, is evil. What do human beings have to do with nuclear destruction at all? In the museum display, there are, after all, no people except bombed people. Americans are not blamed. Not even Japan's wartime leaders are implicated by the jars of pickled tumors; and this possibly because the evil of mass murder is better understood on their side of the Pacific than it has ever been in this country. Japan's present silence on Hiroshima is the supreme understatement of our time. Only an American would think that silence means nothing.

Though the Japanese sense of national apology is complex and at times difficult to understand, one thing we can probably say is that it is profound in comparison to ours. By winning the "Good War" we lost much goodness, even though our false sense of righteousness blinds us to the loss. Self-congratulation has helped to erase our memories of atrocity. To our way of thinking, the atrocities simply did not exist. Why else would the radio commentator Paul Harvey declare that God gave us the first nuclear weapon because no other nation on earth was righteous enough to use it correctly? One can't help but wonder if Harvey's God is also the one inserted into the Pledge of Allegiance after the war, when "one nation, with liberty and justice for all" became "one nation, *under God,* with liberty and justice for all."

The addition to the original Pledge of Allegiance, some will say, is an improvement because it clarifies the divine nature of our state and the very point of our unity. Having made the Japanese renounce their divinity, we apparently feel a bit more upbeat about ours. But if we are united by this godliness and even made free and just by it (as the Pledge can be interpreted), then we must be free enough and righteous enough to ask the overwhelming question: Who sent the Japanese-Americans to the wasteland?

Even God has only one vote in a democracy such as ours. Our mistakes should be recognized as our own, and so must our regrets and apologies. The decision to evacuate the Japanese from the West Coast and southern Arizona was made by people—not by evanescent powers such as those lurking behind passive-voiced Reaganisms like "mistakes were made." If we as a democratic people have anything to congratulate ourselves about, it is not our ability to obliterate Hiroshima and Nagasaki but our power to pass a bill that redresses a national mistake, that makes us a bit nobler because of its apology.

Wilshire Bus

by Hisaye Yamamoto

How does anti-Asian prejudice affect the way Asian Americans view each other? In this story, set in Los Angeles some years after World War II, a Japanese-American woman has a surprising reaction to anti-Chinese bigotry. She hears comments by a man she classifies as a somatotonic, or powerfully built and aggressive person.

Wilshire Boulevard begins somewhere near the heart of downtown Los Angeles and, except for a few digressions scarcely worth mentioning, goes straight out to the edge of the Pacific Ocean. It is a wide boulevard and traffic on it is fairly fast. For the most part, it is bordered on either side with examples of the recent stark architecture which favors a great deal of glass. As the boulevard approaches the sea, however, the landscape becomes a bit more pastoral, so that the university and the soldiers' home there give the appearance of being huge country estates.

Esther Kuroiwa got to know this stretch of territory quite well while her husband Buro was in one of the hospitals at the soldiers' home. They had been married less than a year when his back, injured in the war, began troubling him again, and he was forced to take three months of treatments at Sawtelle before he was able to go back to work. During this time, Esther was permitted to visit him twice a week and she usually took the yellow bus out on Wednesdays because she did not know the first thing about driving and because her friends were not able to take her except on Sundays. She always enjoyed the long bus ride very much because her seat companions usually turned out to be amiable, and if they did not, she took vicarious pleasure in gazing out at the almost unmitigated elegance along the fabulous street.

It was on one of these Wednesday trips that Esther committed a grave sin of omission which caused her later to burst into tears and which caused her acute discomfort for a long time afterwards whenever something reminded her of it.

The man came on the bus quite early and Esther noticed him briefly as he entered because he said gaily to the driver, "You robber. All you guys do is take money from me every day, just for giving me a short lift!"

Handsome in a red-faced way, greying, medium of height, and dressed in a dark grey sport suit with a yellow-and-black flowered shirt, he said this in a nice, resonant, carrying voice which got the response of a scattering of titters from the bus. Esther, somewhat amused and classifying him as a somatotonic, promptly forgot about him. And since she was sitting alone in the first regular seat, facing the back of the driver and the two front benches facing each other, she returned to looking out the window.

At the next stop, a considerable mass of people piled on and the last two climbing up were an elderly Oriental man and his wife. Both were neatly and somberly clothed and the woman, who wore her hair in a bun and carried a bunch of yellow and dark red chrysanthemums, came to sit with Esther. Esther turned her head to smile a greeting (well, here we are, Orientals together on a bus), but the woman was watching, with some concern, her husband who was asking directions of the driver.

His faint English was inflected in such a way as to

make Esther decide he was probably Chinese, and she noted that he had to repeat his question several times before the driver could answer it. Then he came to sit in the seat across the aisle from his wife. It was about then that a man's voice, which Esther recognized soon as belonging to the somatotonic, began a loud monologue in the seat just behind her. It was not really a monologue, since he seemed to be addressing his seat companion, but this person was not heard to give a single answer. The man's subject was a figure in the local sporting world who had a nice fortune invested in several of the shining buildings the bus was just passing.

"He's as tight-fisted as they make them, as tight-fisted as they come," the man said. "Why, he wouldn't give you the sweat of his . . ." He paused here to rephrase his metaphor, ". . . wouldn't give you the sweat off his palm!"

And he continued in this vein, discussing the private life of the famous man so frankly that Esther knew he must be quite drunk. But she listened with interest, wondering how much of this diatribe was true, because the public legend about the famous man was emphatic about his charity. Suddenly, the woman with the chrysanthemums jerked around to get a look at the speaker and Esther felt her giving him a quick but thorough examination before she turned back around.

"So you don't like it?" the man inquired, and it was a moment before Esther realized that he was now directing his attention to her seat neighbor.

"Well, if you don't like it," he continued, "why don't you get off this bus, why don't you go back where you came from? Why don't you go back to China?"

Then, his voice growing jovial, as though he were

certain of the support of the bus in this at least, he embroidered on this theme with a new eloquence, "Why don't you go back to China, where you can be coolies working in your bare feet out in the rice fields? You can let your pigtails grow and grow in China. Alla samee, mama, no tickee no shirtee. Ha, pretty good, no tickee no shirtee!"

He chortled with delight and seemed to be looking around the bus for approval. Then some memory caused him to launch on a new idea "Or why don't you go back to Trinidad? They got Chinks running the whole she-bang in Trinidad. Every place you go in Trinidad . . ."

As he talked on, Esther, pretending to look out the window, felt the tenseness in the body of the woman beside her. The only movement from her was the trembling of the chrysanthemums with the motion of the bus. Without turning her head, Esther was also aware that a man, a mild-looking man with thinning hair and glasses, on one of the front benches was smiling at the woman and shaking his head mournfully in sympathy, but she doubted whether the woman saw.

Esther herself, while believing herself properly annoyed with the speaker and sorry for the old couple, felt quite detached. She found herself wondering whether the man meant her in his exclusion order or whether she was identifiably Japanese. Of course, he was not sober enough to be interested in such fine distinctions, but it did matter, she decided, because she was Japanese, not Chinese, and therefore in the present case immune. Then she was startled to realize that what she was actually doing was gloating over the fact that the drunken man had specified the Chinese as the unwanted.

Briefly, there bobbled on her memory the face of an

elderly Oriental man whom she had once seen from a streetcar on her way home from work. (This was not long after she had returned to Los Angeles from the concentration camp in Arkansas and been lucky enough to get a clerical job with the Community Chest.) The old man was on a concrete island at Seventh and Broadway, waiting for his streetcar. She had looked down on him benignly as a fellow Oriental, from her seat by the window, then been suddenly thrown for a loop by the legend on a large lapel button on his jacket. I AM KOREAN, said the button.

Heat suddenly rising to her throat, she had felt angry, then desolate and betrayed. True, reason had returned to ask whether she might not, under the circumstances, have worn such a button herself. She had heard rumors of I AM CHINESE buttons. So it was true then; why not I AM KOREAN buttons, too? Wryly, she wished for an I AM JAPANESE button, just to be able to call the man's attention to it, "Look at me!" But perhaps the man didn't even read English, perhaps he had been actually threatened, perhaps it was not his doing—his solicitous children perhaps had urged him to wear the badge.

Trying now to make up for her moral shabbiness, she turned towards the little woman and smiled at her across the chrysanthemums, shaking her head a little to get across her message (don't pay any attention to that stupid old drunk, he doesn't know what he's saying, let's take things like this in our stride). But the woman, in turn looking at her, presented a face so impassive yet cold, and eyes so expressionless yet hostile, that Esther's overture fell quite flat.

Okay, okay, if that's the way you feel about it, she thought to herself. Then the bus made another stop and she heard the man proclaim ringingly, "So clear out, all of you, and remember to take every last one of your slant-eyed pickaninnies with you!" This was his final advice as he stepped down from the middle door. The bus remained at the stop long enough for Esther to watch the man cross the street with a slightly exploring step. Then, as it started up again, the bespectacled man in front stood up to go and made a clumsy speech to the Chinese couple and possibly to Esther. "I want you to know," he said, "that we aren't all like that man. We don't all feel the way he does. We believe in an America that is a melting pot of all sorts of people. I'm originally Scotch and French myself." With that, he came over and shook the hand of the Chinese man.

"And you, young lady," he said to the girl behind Esther, "you deserve a Purple Heart or something for having to put up with that sitting beside you."

Then he, too, got off.

The rest of the ride was uneventful and Esther stared out the window with eyes that did not see. Getting off at last at the soldiers' home, she was aware of the Chinese couple getting off after her, but she avoided looking at them. Then, while she was walking towards Buro's hospital very quickly, there arose in her mind some words she had once read and let stick in her craw: People say, do not regard what he says, now he is in liquor. Perhaps it is the only time he ought to be regarded.

These words repeated themselves until her saving detachment was gone every bit and she was filled once again in her life with the infuriatingly helpless, insidiously sickening sensation of there being in the world nothing solid she could put her finger on, nothing solid she could come to grips with, nothing solid she could sink her teeth into, nothing solid.

When she reached Buro's room and caught sight of

his welcoming face, she ran to his bed and broke into sobs that she could not control. Buro was amazed because it was hardly her first visit and she had never shown such weakness before, but solving the mystery handily, he patted her head, looked around smugly at his roommates, and asked tenderly, "What's the matter? You've been missing me a whole lot, huh?" And she, finally drying her eyes, sniffed and nodded and bravely smiled and answered him with the question, yes, weren't women silly?

Trains at Night

by Alberto Alvaro Ríos

Historically, anti-Asian prejudice has not been limited to the United States. Sometime in the 1930s, the president of Mexico ordered the arrest and expulsion of all the Chinese in that country. The incident was not widely reported, but was remembered by the writer's mother-in-law, who watched as the Chinese in her town were herded onto trains one night. This story imaginatively explores how the expulsion order might have affected one Chinese man, his family, and his neighbors.

Mr. Lee, as he transferred chicken feed from the large bin to his everyday pitcher, noticed how the dust rose from the seeds, how steam rises from a landscape, cold, or hot from a white cup of *café con leche,* how smoke rises from a casual backyard fire, how a soul is given up from a sick man. He did not take meaning from this, it was not instruction to him. He simply saw it.

However, when the soldiers came, he had wished possession of that capability, of effecting a rising beyond his own body, of leaving it for them to take, and thereby not feeling what they would do to him, which was unimaginable.

He saw the moment of his imagined escape everywhere, in everything, in the rising of smoke from a cigarette, in a flock of sparrows taking flight. Even, he thought, in the sound of a song let go from the mouth, a whistled aria. That a note of music should take its rightful place with the birds.

He wished it equally for all of them, but his wish did not work very well. The soldiers rounded up all the Chinese they could find, in a day and a night, without warning or manners, without explanation, by neighbor's direction and by rumor and by store sign. Who could have thought this is what would happen, said the townspeople afterward.

But a soldier is a soldier, and who could say no to a soldier's voice? A brown suit like that takes a man, and turns him into his parts. He is nobody's son anymore.

They are always there, without birth and without death, these soldiers. Nobody could say where a soldier comes from. Or who his teachers are, or what they must look like. Where are manners such that a loud step, a stiff neck, a salute in place of the rightful shaking of a hand are marks of grace? Without the hand offered, where is the chance of agreement? Where is the chance of understanding what another has been through by the feeling of roughness in his palm?

Mr. Lee was married with his body and in his heart for a thousand years to Jesusita, married because of, he would shrug his shoulders, who can say? It was like the workings, the intestines, of an opera, he would suggest, and were they not, the two of them, worthy singers in the plot? She would shake her head at him and say she did not understand.

But she did. Not in the way he said it, but she understood in some other way, in the words spoken by his face, clearly what he said.

Mr. Lee was glad that she herself was not Chinese, today. He was glad that she did not look like she needed to be taken away to the trains. He was glad that she did not look like she could profit from a stay in the place where the train would go. Wherever that was, and whatever it meant. To the landscape at the end of the tracks.

And Mr. Lee was glad that his daughters looked like their mother. That he had not given them on their faces a ticket for the train, had not attached it to them so that they would not lose it, the way one might pin a child's mitten to her jacket. In that way, he was happy not to have been able to provide for them. To have been an unfit father, only in this way. Only today.

The Twenties were over now and things had seemed to be getting better, the Revolution, the Depression: it was all over. But to climb out of something like that a country has to grab a hold of something else, some foothold to lift itself, something to step on. That is what this new decade was for, and that is what the Chinese were for, said the President.

Like Mr. Lee he had said this not in regular words, but with some other part of himself. Something equally understandable, equally forceful.

These kinds of nights happen as one would imagine: the President gets indigestion after a meal of bad fish and spoiled butter, a suspect wheel of cheese. He tries to do something, he tries the carbonating powders.

And more. In pain he orders the arrest of all Chinese in the country and their deportation back to China. Who would complain, after all, or who would complain any louder than anyone else, since there were so many voices of complaint for so many things.

It could have been someone else, the Germans, or people from the United States, the *norteamericanos*, but what was the use. People thought the Chinese were beginning to own everything, and there were just enough of them. In truth, it was that their store signs stood out so much, and their faces. In truth, which everybody knew, there were many other choices, but this one was the quickest.

There were the people in Alamos, for example, who lived next to the great silver mine. The ones who ran the operation, at home they had silver everything, silver broom covers, brooms themselves made of silver, and silver on the pillars holding up their houses. Anything to which silver might be added was fashionable there.

But to get them to give it up, well, that was a different thing.

His four daughters cried when they heard what was happening, and cried when they heard the soldiers getting closer. Jesusita did what she could.

In those days the family lived in Los Apóstoles. twelve row houses, or rather, twelve row rooms, owned by Don Lázaro, who did not worry about things very much, and who when asked said that he most certainly did not rent to the Chinese. With what he charged, he said, one could hardly call it rent.

That there were twelve apartments gave rise to both the humor of the name and the mathematics of a problem. Since they were all built at once and were identical, if one problem arose, there were as if by magic twelve. It was a simple and devastating equation for Don Lázaro, who did not always put much stock in the laws of multiplication.

Through the years, each of these quarters began to take on an individual aspect, as Don Lázaro approached each problem as something different from the one before and the one after. He did not, after all, want to insult anyone by not giving them the consideration of listening to their particular problem. Nor, for that matter, did he wish to offend them by turning down a *café con leche* as he listened. He was a good listener, and sometimes he would offer to boil the milk for the second cup of coffee. And he gave each problem its own solution.

But at the very least, twelve similar-looking yards occupied the space behind these apartments, each with a small fence, or some such barrier. And those who knew their own yard knew their neighbor's.

It was night by now, and as the soldiers came and knocked at the first house, Jesusita took her husband into the next yard, and so on down as the soldiers knocked in sequence, as only soldiers with their peculiar efficiency would do.

There were enough garbage cans and compost heaps, enough odd noises by disturbed dogs and grizzled cats, that Jesusita was able to move her husband with some ease. Not the least reason was the irregular rule of geometry, which stated that a small garbage heap was a large mountain to a lazy man. These soldiers were tired already from so much work in the afternoon.

The seven soldiers in the vicinity did not equal one mother calling her child to dinner here. A mother knows how to find a child.

When the soldiers reached the last apartment, Jesusita, who had said she was bringing in laundry, brought her husband back to their rooms, and in through the back door.

His four daughters had said when the soldiers knocked that he was not there, and had not been there for some time, and that they did not know where he was or when he would return, and then shrugged their shoulders.

It figures, said the lieutenant, or the captain, or whatever he was, these Chinese, after all. His voice was a deep voice, and too loud.

The daughters said nothing and went about their business, and at that cue the soldier *harrumphed* and did the same, saying something vague, if you see him, well, you know then, call us, and the daughters replied also with something vague, of course, all right then.

When they left, Jesusita brought her husband in and they all helped to hide him inside the cabinet of the radio, a Ward's "Airline" model, with the word "Heterodyne" underneath. It was a brown piece of furniture, part Greek columns and part lyre in decoration. Before they moved the radio back against the wall, they all looked at him, with the radio tubes and wires all above his head.

He looked like something from the movies, something from a Saturday morning, and they wanted to laugh and cry at the same time. And they heard him say, this cannot be happening. And as they looked at him, they saw that he was right. This was not like doing the laundry or preparing the evening meal. This was nothing they knew. This was after all something from the movies. But it was as if the manager had locked the doors of the theater, and they had to live with this beast.

No one saw Mr. Lee for many years. He did not live here anymore, his family said. But they were not sad. He lived in between the bed sheets and in the bathroom. He fit into the small spaces of the house, and did not eat much.

The soldiers never came back to look for him, but then again there was nothing to look for. Everyone in the town knew that he had disappeared. A pity, they would say, *que lástima*. He was such a smart man.

But times changed, and every now and then people saw him, slowly.

They were not surprised. They understood something of how a thing could happen and not happen. There had been nothing in the newspapers or on the radio about that singular night. They understood how Mr. Lee could be gone and still be here. There was no mystery in seeing something that did not exist. The government had taught them well, and they were good citizens. There were, they knew, many kinds of ghosts.

The rounding up of the Chinese lasted only the one night, as long as the President's heartburn. They loaded them, as people later told each other even in public, into boxcars and open cattle and cotton cars. All over the country the soldiers looked for them, but especially a little farther north, along the border, where they might have been heard by the people on the other side, who might have tried to do something.

Many of the wives who had grown up in this town went with their men, to live in China. They took their children, too, and something or other in their arms. Some of them later came back, and some did not. They were not treated well. But such a thing was not a new life, and they were used to it. Being treated well was not much of a measure for anything anymore.

Not all of the Chinese left, however, and Mr. Lee was not the only one to be hidden. Some men had been dressed like women, and like animals, which was a gypsy trick. And none of them was seen for many years. There was a yipping at the moon some nights during this time, recognizable as coyotes in any other decade, but some townspeople said it was the Chinese. By this they did not mean that they were still in the animal disguises they had worn, but, rather, it was a remark about the quality of voice they heard.

It was a sound reminiscent of the German man, Mr. Luder, whose wife Margarita had died in childbirth along with the child. In the daytime he had a business in clocks, something regular, but every night he slept on the grave of his wife and child, and he wept.

The business later failed, and all he could do was to sleep on that stone and dirt, or walk around the town getting ready to sleep. This walking toward sleep became his job. People, in fact, had sometimes heard Mr. Luder's sobbing, and thought it was coyotes, and later the sounds of the Chinese. It was a sound many animals shared.

Some time later, as many Chinese had made their way up into Arizona, some of them would be mistaken again, this time for Japanese, and taken away once more. They were returned, but again without the courtesy of manners.

When the government later rounded up the Yaqui Indians, they did it the other way around. They could not capture the men. But the women and children who came down from the mountains to trade goods were easy enough to take.

This time they put the women and children in trains, the old trick of how to catch the men, and sent them to the Yucatán just like that. Traveling was dangerous then, as the Yaquis took up the attacking of all the trains in the region, first to try to get their families back and then later out of anger. The Yaquis, many people said, were vicious.

Mr. Lee, the townspeople remarked regularly, was very smart, but by smart they meant a great deal more, which they could not say. He was rumored not so much to be Chinese, but to have had a gypsy father himself, who had shown him the ways of other worlds, who had given him the singular ability to live well in a radio. By now they had heard the story of that night from Jesusita. *In our radio,* she said to them, *looking like a Martian.*

Everyone had laughed when Jesusita told the story, but not too hard. Of course, they thought, with a look each to the other. Of course. He was not, after all, of this place.

When Mr. Lee walked along the path between the black walnut trees lining the streets, it was clear now that he had made his place. That the government had not been able to take him, no matter what the law. That he, because of his head that lit up with tubes, knew something more than the law.

They laughed, but not too hard, and they called on him for advice when they were in trouble, because he would understand. They were a little scared of him, of course, because he knew something about things. He knew the underbelly and the tomorrow and yesterday of things, he knew their opposites and their half-turns. He knew the radio, after all, from the inside out.

He was like Mr. Luder, they sometimes said. He knew about life. He knew about it as if he had walked the perimeter of a park, and thereby gauged something of the dimensions of a neat lawn and the heights of the eucalyptus trees.

And Mr. Lee's pronunciation of words, unlike the laws of the Presidents, never changed, a little stilted even after so many years, a little wrong: it showed that he understood their language better than they did, that he spoke correctly. There was something wrong in this place and in these days, and they heard it in Mr. Lee's accent. He would talk, strange-like, and they knew he was right, about anything, about the weather.

The *wedder*, he would say, and they would understand. And when he smoked, they would think they sometimes saw him, some part of him still hiding a little in the cloud.

Visiting Home

poem by Kevin Young

*This poem recalls an African-American
family's displacement from their Southern
home. In the poem, an unnamed person
(probably the writer) is addressed by his
grandmother and two uncles. How does
this family's experience resemble the
Wakatsuki family's experience?*

for Keith

   Sunnyman:
look there   past
those bitter figs
in the pasture   you can
5 barely make it out now
but all that you see
all that green   once
was ours

   Mama Lucille:
10 it must have been the summer
before DaDa seemed taller
than everyone   the year your Uncle
Sunnyman was born   the season Keith
stole all your father's well-worn
15 hard-won   wooden marbles
from a drawer   and shot
them from a slingshot
at the cows   what slow
moving barns
20 they were

Keith:
DaDa left out in the heat
his share of mornings   only
to return from the market
25   in Plaisance with nothing   a hog maybe
sometimes a good sow
but we never had enough
to raise it on   so he slaughtered
what we couldn't keep
30   gave up the best meat

though he might save
some pigsfeet
for us

Mama Lucille:
35   when whitemen came with fear
in the night
they told DaDa he had
   to leave
   that was right
40   before the war
and land was so tight
people just got crazy

the mosquitoes that June flew big
as horses

45   we burnt green wood
and the smoke kept them away

Keith:
the old house stood
about three four mile across the way
50   you know
where the road runs now

it was one of those
old shotgun homes
you could have blasted
55 right straight through it
in one door and out another

but no one never did

Sunnyman:
no one really told me
60 when it was   they tore
the empty thing down
Mama had waited a long time
in that house
been so many things
65 mother wife sister queen
guess it wasn't long after DaDa passed on
from that oversized heart
of his   that she weaned me
in this new place   boy, consider yourself
70 warned: his condition
runs in our family
like you wouldn't believe

Mama Lucille:
it was sunny and my skin ripened
75 to oranges   I didn't
even have a proper dress
for the funeral
me being pregnant
with Robert and all
80 so I wore the one with daisies
figured DaDa would like that
just as much   wasn't nearly
as hot that way
but was it ever sunny

85   *Keith:*
    there never was a will

    DaDa didn't believe in one
    he just said the earth
    was for whoever needed it most
90   said we never could own
    the land   we just ate
    out an ever-emptying hand

    some pale man
    at the funeral
95   said the X
    by the deed was his
    and not DaDa's   and he
    could prove it
    said we'd have to move
100   or fight him
    and the entire state
    of Louisiana

    of course we let it go

    Sunnyman:
105   folks say this land will never be Young again
    that we have lived too long without
    so many things that having
    seems too hard   but there's one thing
    we can never forget: how the land we were
110   promised is gone how home for us
    is wherever we're not

from Unto the Sons

by Gay Talese

Italian-American Gay Talese grew up during World War II, with ties to a country viewed—like Japan—as "the enemy." As you read this excerpt from his memoir, compare his life to Jeanne Wakatsuki Houston's, and compare Talese's father to hers.

I saw myself always as an alien, an outsider, a drifter who, like shipwrecked sailors, had arrived by accident. I felt different from my young friends in almost every way, different in the cut of my clothes, the food in my lunch box, the music I heard at home on the record player, the ideas and inner thoughts I revealed on those rare occasions when I was open and honest.

I was olive-skinned in a freckle-faced town, and I felt unrelated even to my parents, especially my father, who was indeed a foreigner—an unusual man in dress and manner, to whom I bore no physical resemblance and with whom I could never identify. Trim and elegant, with wavy dark hair and a small rust-colored moustache, he spoke English with an accent and received letters bearing strange-looking stamps.

These letters sometimes contained snapshots of soldiers wearing uniforms with insignia and epaulets unlike any I had seen on the recruitment posters displayed throughout the island. They were my uncles and cousins, my father explained to me quietly one day early in World War II, when I was ten; they were fighting in the Italian army, and—it was unnecessary for him to add—their enemy included the government of the United States.

I became increasingly sensitive to this fact when I sat through the newsreels each week at the local cinema; next to my unknowing classmates, I watched with private horror the destruction by Allied bombers of mountain villages and towns in southern Italy to which I was ancestrally linked through a historically ill-timed relationship with my Italian father. At any moment I half expected to see up on the screen, gazing down at me from a dust-covered United States Army truck filled with disheveled Italian prisoners being guarded at gunpoint, a sad face that I could identify from one of my father's snapshots.

My father, on the other hand, seemed to share none of my confused sense of patriotism during the war years. He joined a citizens' committee of shore patrolmen who kept watch along the waterfront at night, standing with binoculars on the boardwalk under the stanchioned lights that on the ocean side were painted black as a precaution against discovery by enemy submarines.

He made headlines in the local newspaper after a popular speech to the Rotary Club in which he reaffirmed his loyalty to the Allied cause, declaring that were he not too old for the draft (he was thirty-nine) he would proudly join the American troops at the front, in a uniform devotedly cut and stitched with his own hands.

Trained as an apprentice tailor in his native village, and later an assistant cutter in a prominent shop in Paris that employed an older Italian cousin, my father arrived in Ocean City circuitously and impulsively at the age of eighteen in 1922 with very little money, an extensive wardrobe, and the outward appearance of a man who knew exactly where he was going, when in fact nothing was further from the truth. He knew no one in town, barely knew the language, and yet, with a self-assurance that has always mystified me, he adjusted to this unusual island as readily as he could cut cloth to fit any size and shape.

Having noticed a "For Sale" sign in the window of a tailor shop in the center of town, my father approached the asthmatic owner, who was desperate to leave the island for the drier climate of Arizona. After a brief negotiation, my father acquired the business and thus began a lengthy, spirited campaign to bring the rakish fashion of the Continental boulevardier to the comparatively continent men of the south Jersey shore.

But after decorating his windows with lantern-jawed mannequins holding cigarettes and wearing Borsalino hats, and draping his counters with bolts of fine imported fabrics—and displaying on his walls such presumably persuasive regalia as his French master tailor's diploma bordered by cherubim and a Greek goddess—my father made so few sales during his first year that he was finally forced to introduce into his shop a somewhat undignified gimmick called the Suit Club.

At the cost of one dollar per week, Suit Club members would print their names and addresses on small white cards and, after placing the cards in unmarked envelopes, would deposit them into a large opaque vase placed prominently atop a velvet-covered table next to a fashion photograph of a dapper man and woman posing with a greyhound on the greensward of an ornate country manor.

Each Friday evening just prior to closing time, my father would invite one of the assembled Suit Club members to close his eyes and pick from the vase a single envelope, which would reveal the name of the fortunate winner of a free suit, to be made from fabric selected by that individual; after two fittings, it would be ready for wearing within a week.

Since as many as three or four hundred people were soon paying a dollar each week to partake in this raffle, my father was earning on each free suit a profit perhaps three times the average cost of a custom-made suit in those days—to say nothing of the additional money he earned when he enticed a male winner into purchasing an extra pair of matching trousers.

But my father's bonanza was abruptly terminated one day in 1928, when an anonymous complaint sent to City Hall, possibly by a rival tailor, charged that the Suit Club was a form of gambling clearly outlawed under the town charter; thus ended for all time my father's full-time commitment to the reputable but precarious life of an artist with a needle and thread. My father did *not* climb down from an impoverished mountain in southern Italy and forsake the glorious lights of Paris and sail thousands of miles to the more opportunistic shores of America to end up as a poor tailor in Ocean City, New Jersey.

So he diversified. Advertising himself as a ladies' furrier who could alter or remodel old coats as well as provide resplendent new ones (which he obtained on consignment from a Russian Jewish immigrant who resided in nearby Atlantic City), my father expanded his store to accommodate a refrigerated fur storage vault and extended the rear of the building to include a dry-cleaning plant overseen by a black Baptist deacon who during Prohibition operated a small side business in bootlegging. Later, in the 1930s, my father added a ladies' dress boutique, having as partner and wife a well-tailored woman who once worked as a buyer in a large department store in Brooklyn. . . .

Quite apart from his patriotic activities with the Ocean City shore patrol throughout World War II, and his pro-American speeches to the local Rotary Club, which would soon elect him its president, my father was silently terrified by the Allied forces' successful invasion of Sicily in 1943 and their inevitable plan to move north up the Italian peninsula against the Nazi and Fascist troops who were encamped in and around the southern region of his birth.

His widowed mother still occupied the Talese family's ancient stone house in the hills with most of my father's kinfolk, except those who were soldiers at the front, associated with the Germans against the advancing Allied ground units and bombers.

The southernmost part of Italy was virtually indefensible, my father conceded to me at breakfast after reading in *The New York Times* about the fall of Sicily; it was the fragile toe of the Italian boot, an exposed area where the slanted farmlands and jagged hills descended from the higher northern peaks and were surrounded almost entirely by unguarded bodies of water. To the east was the Ionian Sea, to the west the Tyrrhenian, and to the southwest was the Strait of Messina, which scarcely separated the southern tip of Italy from the island of Sicily.

Although my father's village—Maida—was sixty-five miles northeast of Messina, it was precariously situated. The curving coastlines of the Ionian and Tyrrhenian seas cut deeply into the mainland, so deeply that Maida's population of thirty-five hundred people was clustered in beige stone houses on the rocky interior of the narrowest part of Italy. The distance between the two coastlines here could be traversed by a motorist in little more than an hour; and adding to Maida's vulnerability to invasion, my father said, was a wide plateau below its western slope that could serve as a passageway or attacking ground for great numbers of troops traveling with heavy equipment. Indeed, this land had already been the scene of a brutal battle between the soldiers of France and Britain during the era of Napoleon Bonaparte.

It happened on a hot July morning in 1806, said my father, whose recounting of history was always accompanied by precise details; it happened after the surprise landing of more than five thousand British troops on the shingly shore of the Tyrrhenian Sea along the outer edge of Maida's plateau.

The British troops were led by a bold American-born officer who was a native of Georgia—General John Stuart, whose property-owning parents in the American South had remained loyal to the crown during the American Revolution. After they had returned to England, young Stuart received a commission as a British officer in 1778. In 1780 he participated in the siege of Charleston, South Carolina; then the invasion of North Carolina and, finally, Virginia, where, severely wounded, he and other red-coated units under Lord Cornwallis surrendered to the Americans at Yorktown in 1781.

After recovering his health and returning to England, Stuart resumed a military career that during the following decades would see him leading British regiments, brigades, and divisions between Flanders and Alexandria in almost constant conflict with the French—culminating, after sailing with his troops from Sicily past the rock of Scylla northward toward that plateau, in the battle of Maida in 1806.

The Italian mainland in 1806 was largely influenced by the Emperor Napoleon Bonaparte, a fact that was not displeasing to a large percentage of Italians. As my father often said, the Italians considered Napoleon more Italian than French because he was descended from a family that had emigrated from northern Italy to Corsica when that island was ruled by the Italian republic of Genoa— which, over the protests of many Corsicans, ceded it to the French shortly before Napoleon's birth in Corsica in 1769.

Among the anti-French Corsican agitators during this time was Napoleon's father, who became resigned to the French occupation of the island only after the leader of the Corsican resistance movement had been forced to flee. As a result of his father's subsequent cooperation and politicking with the French administrators, the younger Napoleon was able to leave Corsica and receive the benefits of a higher education in continental France. And yet during his school years and swift rise through the ranks of the French army, Napoleon continued to spell his surname in the Italian style, "Buonaparte," even after he had been appointed a brigadier general at the age of twenty-four in 1793.

It was in this same year that the British officer John Stuart became a lieutenant colonel at thirty-four; but as my father pointed out, it was much more difficult to move up within the British officer corps than the French because France was then involved with its Reign of Terror, and there were frequent vacancies created at the top of the French military establishment because of the many defections, expulsions, and even executions of aristocratic French officers.

It was during this very same year of 1793, in fact, that the French beheaded King Louis XVI and his wife, Marie Antoinette. The act shocked royal rulers around the world, but it was mourned with more personal passion in the palace at Naples, the capital city of the southern Italian kingdom, where the throne was occupied by Queen Marie Caroline (sister of the guillotined Marie Antoinette) and the Bourbon king Ferdinand, a member of a branch of the same dynasty as the fallen French king.

In addition to the sadness and anger in Naples there were grave feelings of insecurity among the ruling elite throughout the Kingdom of Southern Italy, because they were aware that in Maida, as in dozens of other villages, secret revolutionary societies were scheming to overthrow the privileged families who had ruled over the hills and farmlands since the Norman conquerors had brought feudalism into southern Italy in the eleventh century.

A Norman castle built in Maida in that century was still standing in the early twentieth, my father told me; and despite its decrepit condition, it was sometimes used when he was a child as a place of incarceration while the accused awaited transfer to a larger prison elsewhere. But the castle's dungeon also served to remind my father how deep-rooted was the medieval mentality of his native land, how enduring were certain of its archaic methods. Indeed, the Maida valley that would be the battleground between Napoleon's musketeers and Stuart's invaders in 1806—the British won the conflict after four ferocious days, and subsequently memorialized it by naming a West London district Maida Vale, after my father's village—had undoubtedly absorbed the blood of two thousand years of warfare, going back to the days of Roman chariots and Hannibal's elephants, of savage Magyar horsemen and Saracen pirates who, sailing toward southern Italy with clarions and trumpets blaring, filled the sunny sky with darts of poison.

While I was always impressed with my father's vivid depiction of history, my attention sometimes wandered during these long and frequently repetitive lectures conducted after dinner amid the soft but often distracting sounds of Puccini and Verdi rising from the scratchy glass records of my father's old Victrola. And yet his intensity made me aware of his almost obsessive need to tell me about himself, to explain and perhaps justify himself as he described his past and traced his odyssey along the Tyrrhenian Sea to Paris and later across the Atlantic Ocean to the Jersey shore, where he now had me as his captive audience. To me he could confess his anxiety and, possibly, guilt, or at the very least expose a side of himself that his tailor's taste for appearances would prevent him from revealing beyond the walls of this mirrored apartment.

Ironically, while I was failing an American history course in parochial school—where I was also subjected to ethnic slurs hurled by a few Irish Catholic boys whose older brothers had just participated in the conquest of Sicily—I was becoming, under my father's tutelage, a reluctant scholar of the history of the southern tip of Italy, which, if my father's worst fears materialized, would soon be blown off the map.

Perhaps that accounted for his determination to enlighten me about it, so that I might survive, as he had, to keep its obscure history alive in the retelling—and to take pride, as well as solace, in associating Italy with the rich chronology preceding its alliance with Nazi Germany.

Lectures on How You Never Lived Back Home

by M. Evelina Galang

Farewell to Manzanar poignantly describes a Japanese-American girl's struggle to create an identity for herself. In this story, a daughter of Filipino immigrants describes her similar struggle a generation later.

You grew up hearing two languages—one you can pull apart, name, slap a series of rules to, twist like clay-dough in a child's hand—the other you cannot explain, you listen and you know. It is a language you understand intuitively—like being able to read the sunrise, the strips of pink and orange, the clumps of uneven clouds, a thin patch of grey and the moon and somehow, without thinking twice, you know what kind of day it will be. You understand like this because you are the first born. First generation. First American. First cousin. First hope.

Back home, one of your grandmothers sewed children's clothing by hand and sold them in an open-air market. The other grandmother raised seven children on her own, gathering them up, hiding them away in the provinces along the sea, away from Japanese soldiers, away from American fighters. Away from war. Your grandmother feared the safety of all her children, especially her young ladies. Your mother survived wartime. She was smart and well-read and ambitious, skipped grades, travelled across the oceans, met your father in Milwaukee, gave up her princess status to be your mother. As a boy, your dad farmed fish out of monsoon-swollen rice paddies, cut school to hitchhike from Pampanga to Rizal just to see MacArthur. Somewhere in his youth, he spied on American GIs and caught on to this notion of democracy, this notion of rights. His rights, his family's rights, the rights of his countrymen. The rights taken first by three hundred years of Spanish rule, then Japanese terror and war, then of course, there were the Americans and their intentions. After sneaking about soldier camps, making friends with a GI from Atlanta, bumming cigarettes from another one from Pasadena, your father worked his way out of those provinces, studied hard at school. He passed his boards, passed immigration, slipped into that ballroom on Racine and Wisconsin, and charmed his way into your mother's life.

They raised you to understand that back home, a young girl serves her parents, lives to please them, fetches her father's slippers and her mother's cups of tea. Back home a young girl learns to embroider fine stitches, learns parlor dances, wears white uniforms at all-girl schools, convent schools. She never crosses her legs or wears skirts above the knee. Back home a girl does not date. She is courted. And when there is a young man present, there is always a chaperon. Young ladies grow up to be young housewives, good mothers, and in their old age, they still behave like obedient daughters.

You, on the other hand, have never had to obey a curfew because of war, never had to tiptoe through your own house, never had to read your books underneath a blanket where no soldier would see. As far as you knew, your curfew was your curfew because Mom and Dad said so. You were raised in suburbia in a split-level house, always in fashion, even when you were only two, dressed in your white lace and pink ribbons, toting your very own parasol. You've never been without heat, without food, without parents. All your life your worries consisted of boys and pimples and overdue books. You had your first boy-girl party when you were five years old, played Pin-the-Tail-on-the-Donkey and kissed Timmy Matasaki underneath the dining room table. You had a bad habit of talking back. You learned how to scream no to your parents, and it didn't matter if you were punished, slapped across the face, sent away to sulk, banished to the kitchen, you still opened your mouth and the words came out.

You grew up pouring chicken soy sauce dishes over beds of steamed rice, never mashing potatoes until you were on your own, eating your meals with a spoon in your right hand, a fork in the left, marvelling at the Americans and how they could balance entire meals on one fork, or the Chinese who could eat bowls of rice with two sticks. Your family roasted pigs on a spit, while next door, the neighbors cooked brats and burgers on electric grills.

From the start, you were a piece that did not fit, never given the chance to be like the rest—the ones with blond hair and red hair and something someone called strawberry. The ones with eyes that change like the ocean—green to blue to seafoam, depending on the color of their sweater. Your eyes have always been black. Your hair dark. Straight. No variety. To the kids at school, you were no different from the other Oriental girl, the one who spoke English with a chopped-up accent. To your aunts and uncles you were turning into a *bratty Americana,* loose like those blond children, mouthy like the kids who ran the streets wild. They worried you might grow up too indelicate for marriage.

Now you are well over twenty-five and still single. The old aunts raise one eyebrow and say, See? But you know, it's because you refuse to settle for less than best. Anyone can get married, you say. You not only tell men off, you ask them out. Recently, you've considered having a child without a father. This attitude bangs up against your mother's heart like the bumpers of two cars when she's parallel parking and the car doesn't fit. Sometimes she looks at you and sighs.

Your home is in Bucktown, Wicker Park, Ravenswood, Illinois, and because you won't admit the fact that what your parents call "back home" has made a place in your house, because you are not white, and still you are not one of them—the foreigners—you continue to displease everyone. Your father's headache is mostly just you. He has been known to throw his hands up, call you stubborn, say *Bahala na!* It's up to you. Your choice. Your responsibility.

Still, in the privacy of your kitchen, you admit you cannot live without your family, your history, this ideal called "your people." You cannot divorce yourself from yourself. You know you are the hyphen in American-born. Your identity scrawls the length and breadth of the page, American-born-girl. American-born-Filipina. Because you have always had one foot planted in the Midwest, one foot floating on the islands, and your arms have stretched across the generations, barely kissing your father's province, your children's future, the dreams your mother has for you. Because you were meant for the better life, whatever that is, been told you mustn't forget where you come from, what others have done for you. Because all your life you've simply been told. Just told. Because a council of ancestors—including a few who are not yet dead, who are not even related to you—haunt you, you do your best. You try. You struggle. And somehow, when you stand in the center of a room, and the others look on, you find yourself acting out your role. Smart American girl, beautiful Filipina, dutiful daughter.

Acknowledgments

Continued from page ii

Chronicle Books: "Trains at Night," from *Pig Cookies* by Alberto Alvaro Ríos. Copyright © 1995 by Alberto Alvaro Ríos. Reprinted by permission of the publisher, Chronicle Books, San Francisco.

William Morrow & Company, Inc.: "Visiting Home," from *Most Way Home* by Kevin Young. Copyright © 1995 by Kevin Young/Fisted Pick Productions. By permission of William Morrow & Company, Inc.

Alfred A. Knopf, Inc.: Excerpt from *Unto the Sons* by Gay Talese. Copyright © 1992 by Gay Talese. Reprinted by permission of Alfred A. Knopf, Inc.

Coffee House Press: "Lectures on How You Never Lived Back Home" is reprinted from *Her Wild American Self* by M. Evelina Galang, Coffee House Press, 1996. Copyright © 1996 by M. Evelina Galang. Used with permission of Coffee House Press.